A.T.S.
COMMANDO

ACTION THRILLER STORY OF
A.T.S.
COMMANDO

RAM VINAYAK

PARTRIDGE
A Penguin Random House Company

To order additional copies of this book, contact
Partridge India
000 800 10062 62
orders.india@partridgepublishing.com

www.partridgepublishing.com/india

CHAPTER - I

For the past one hour, Abhijeet has been standing on the deck holding railing of an Indian Navy ship, which has been converted into a training vessel for elite Marine Commandoes known as MARCOS. Monsoons' drizzles continue to sensualize his face with a strange pleasure. He wants to enjoy every moments of the last day with INS Abhimanyu, which has transformed him into a killing machine during the last one years of commando training. He could feel the impact of rough sea waves hitting the ship. His mind is trying to flow with the chirpings of seagulls mixed with the rippling sound of sea waves. He wants to shake out all those hardships he has undergone during the last two years training period i.e. one year at Maharashtra Police Academy at Nasik and subsequent one year commandos training of MARCOS, which has been termed as one of the best commando training organizations in the world. Tomorrow, he is going to join Anti-Terrorism Squad (ATS) Mumbai.

Suddenly, the drizzling turns into rain pour, but he does not move keep on standing like an iron statue. He has muscular body with 5'11" height, broad shoulders, round face and slightly dark complexion. His round brownish eyes, flat nose and wide chin with thick magnum moustache make him look like hard core cop. Oblivious of the rain pour getting furious with howling gale, events starts to unfold in his mind. . Recollecting the past two year's events, he thinks, How *fast the time has passed? It was only two years back, when he entered the Maharashtra Police Academy for the training of Deputy Superintendent of Police. He still vividly remember the speech delivered by the Commandant of the Police Academy on the first day of their training:*

> *"Gentleman Cadets, myself Vishwajeet Shinde, Commandant of your Academy. First of all congratulate you for having been selected for the elite position of Dy. Superintendent of Police in Maharashtra Police, which is one of the oldest police force in the country and has distinguished record for its bravery, great values, devotion, intelligence and loyalty. This Academy has imparted professional training to thousands of officers, who are servicing the Police Force with their best of ability. Your Academy has state of art facilities for latest Information Technology, simulation for weapon use. We have highly trained faculty and Instructor to help you understand and use complex methodology and give you physical training which will make you professionally capable to contain crime and terror so that the people of Maharashtra can have a safe and peaceful life. All of you will have great responsibility and obligation towards the society and I am sure you will bring pride to the Police Force." He paused for few moment, cleared his throat and continued;*

> *"During your training period you will be studying Indian Penal Code, Code of Criminal Procedure, Evidence Act, Constitution of Human Rights, Law,*

Forensic Science & Medicine, Investigation Theory, Maintenance of Public Peace & Order, Criminology & Crime Prevention, Investigation Practical, Police Manual and Police Station Management & Crime Control."

"Tomorrow, your training will start and next eleven months training period will bring best out of you. I wish all the best for you. Jai Maharashtra!"

Being an athlete, marshal art black belt holder during his college time and coming from a farmer's family, it was so comfortable for him to pass out with gold medal. It was only after his selection for Anti-Terrorism Squad when he was sent to INS Abhimanyu for MARCOS training and it became a real tough going. Nine months training at INS Abhimanyu and subsequently three months spent with three different commandoes training centres will remain embedded in his memory for ever. From tomorrow, his career with ATS will begin, opening a new chapter in his life.

In view of the sudden spurt of terrorist activities in Maharashtra, especially in the financial city of Mumbai, it has been decided by the Home Ministry to expand and modernize the Anti Terrorism Squad (ATS) wing of the State in a bid to check burgeoning menace of terrorism and to counter their threat to the people & infrastructures of Maharashtra. It is proposed to enhance capability of ATS, making it an elite anti-terrorism agency at par with the best agencies of the world. In view of the major expansion and restructuring of ATS, its Head Office has been shifted from its present location to an independent eight storeys building, situated in an excluded location. The premises of ATS Head

Office is surrounded by a 10' high concrete boundary walls, with CCTV cameras and alarm systems installed all along the walls.

Basement and ground floor of the building have been kept reserve for parking of vehicles, which have been issued parking permission by the Security. The building is built in the premises of about 4000 sq. mtrs. Functioning of the office is divided in number of sections, e.g. Administrative, Finance, Legal Cell, Information and Communication Technology, Training, conference halls, Dinning halls separately for officers and other cadres & staff members, pantries on each floor, Interrogation Rooms, Control Room, Maintenance Section, Strong rooms for keeping weapons and ammunition for emergent needs. There are rooms for drivers and Security Staff. Each and every corner of the building is covered by CCTV surveillance. Before entering the building everyone has to pass through security clearance at three stages. In the first stage, everyone has to swipe ID card through slot of an electronic machine, then has to pass through scanning system and finally physical frisking is done on everybody.

There is an exclusive transport section, which manages the fleet of vehicles, equipped with telecommunication system for the use of ATS personnel during operation, and plying of buses for pickup and dropping of staff and other members. Since the building is spread over large area, there are eight lifts in the building, out of which only four lifts are for use of staff and the remaining three lifts are reserved for use of senior officers, and other purposes for some security reasons and maintaining confidentiality. One heavy duty lift is to be used as service lift. There is an exclusive parking lot for operation vehicles.

The Control Room, from where all activities of ATS are monitored, has been designed and installed with the latest Information and Communication Technology equipment and devices by an American Company. Control Room has an integrated communication system connecting all the units of ATS.

A giant dish antennas have been installed on the top of the HO building to have a dedicated communication system through satellites. The Control Room is a big hall with dozens of monitors and screens for conducting video conferencing and monitoring purposes. Activities at all the sensitive areas of Mumbai can be watched and monitored through these monitors. Control Room, with the help of a dedicated satellite channel, can have surveillance of any area of the State. Even the registration number of any vehicles can be read through satellite. Two Expert Trainers from the American firm, who have installed the whole system, have been retained to train Computer & Software Engineers, Staff and Officers to operate and maintain the system efficiently. One Intelligence Officer from SWAT, USA is also there to impart training to ATS staff to coordinate with other national and international Intelligence Agencies in order to gather, compile and analyse data regarding terrorist activities.

Vishnu Madhik, DSP who is a training mate of Abhijeet, is given overall charge for the Control Room, which will be managed by Software Engineers, Inspector and

Sub-Inspector level officers and Assistants. Only authorized personnel are allowed to enter the Control Room. Vishnu is reporting directly to an IPS Officer of Commissioner of Police rank. There is one glass chamber for Vishnu from where he can watch all activities of the Control Room, but for video Conferencing he will need to come out or go to an adjoining conference room, where a big electronic screen is installed. Fourth floor of the building is meant for Control Room, two Conference Rooms, Office of Commissioner of Police and his staff.

All administrative and supporting offices including Finance, HR, Maintenance and Security have been accommodated on the first floor. Second Floor contains Dining Hall, food catering Section and Stores.

Third floor is meant for training section, Legal Cell and library.

Fifth and sixth floors are for field operation office, Conference Rooms, Interrogation Rooms, strong room for weapons and ammunition.

Seventh floor has offices of Chief of ATS and other top IPS Officers and their staff. There is separate dining room for the Chief, Commissioners and other Director level officials.

Eighth floor is practically left vacant for future expansion plans.

All windows of fourth, fifth, sixth and seven floors are bullet proof and fitted with blinds. An advance system has been adopted for Information and Communication so as to prevent hacking of any computers or interception of communication.

Abhijeet, who is reporting to an IPS Officer Rahul Rana has been given cabin on 5th floor. His boss SP Rahul

Rana is also a young officers, hardly four years older to Abhijeet and he is very friendly with his colleagues. After his IPS training, he has been trained at SWAT, Los Angle for six months. He has led number of operations successfully and received Police Award for the same. He enjoys good reputation in the organization. He is married with one kid.

Abhijeet heads a Field Operation team of a dozen commandoes to carry out the field operations to deal with the terrorists and handling situations where there is thin line between life and death. All new comers are briefed for two weeks regarding code of conducts, secrecy and confidentiality to be observed while they are associated with ATS. Abhijeet and Vishnu and other officers have been provided single and family accommodation as per their marital status in the Police Line.

Every moment in the Office add to their learning while sharing their experiences, conducting case study and intelligence analysis which enhance their intuition level. Many times, they have to go by their intuition in critical moments.

CHAPTER - II

It's now more than one month since Abhijeet has joined ATS. Abhijeet along with two constable and one Sub-Inspector, while on night duty, is out for patrolling on Highway. SP Rana comes on line and says, "Abhijeet, we have received a message from Intelligence Bureau that two suspected terrorist are staying in a building in Goregaon East area. The tip off has come from one of the RAW Agents, who has been trailing them. The Agent is putting on dark blue jeans and red colour strips T-shirt and can be contact outside the building."

Abhijeet says, "OK Sir, I am heading to the location along with my team and will be there within 20 minutes."

Parking his vehicle away from the building, Abhijeet walks down towards the building and spots the Agent standing at the bus stand, where few commuters are waiting for the bus. When they make eye contact with each other, the Agent brings his mobile close to his ears and pretend as if he is speaking to someone over mobile and says, "Listen, put 4.3 mm size rods on the right side of the window and finish the job urgently, it is already too late", and walks away continuing talking on the mobile. It was enough for Abhijeet to get the message that the suspects are on fourth floor in the flat, which has third window from the right side and action need to be taken urgently before the suspect leave building.

Abhijeet returns to his vehicle and contacting with Rana over wireless says, "Sir, we got the location of the objects. Please send a team of Commandoes with all gadgets and bullet-proofs. These suspects must be armed and may put up resistance. Operation needs to be confined to the room to avoid any residents of the building getting hurt during the operation, if leads to shoot out."

After few minutes, SP Rana comes on the line, "Abhijeet, I have spoken to the Chief. he wants them alive for extracting vital information. I am sure, you can do it. Reinforcement with necessary gadgets (weapons, ammunitions and bullet proof) is reaching you any moment. Put coverage from all side. Chief is speaking to Commissioner (Traffic) to hold traffic on the front road of the flat for operation. When you are ready to move, streets lights will go off. Take stairs."

"We will try to take them alive."

Two more vehicles of ATS arrive and parked near his vehicle. Back door of both the vehicles open. About ten commandoes, in their full preparedness, came down. Abhijeet and his three colleagues also put on bulletproof and take out loaded automatic guns from the vehicles. All of them put on night visions. Abhijeet contacting Rana says, "Sir, get the traffic block from both direction and street lights to go off. We are ready to move."

Within one minute, traffic from both sides stops coming. Abhijeet addressing four commandoes says, "You may cover the building from all sides. Nobody should escape."

Then addressing remaining commandoes he says, "The moment street lights goes off, action will start."

The moment street lights goes off, all commandos, with lightning speed, enter the building through main entrance and within no time they reach fourth floor. Two of the commandos with the blow of their kicks blast the doors open. They find four persons sitting around a table, perhaps planning for something. One of them tries to pull gun, but a bullet from automatic gun fitted with silencer penetrates his head. Remaining three persons raise their hands to surrender. Abhijeet sees one of them is chewing something and next moment he crumbles down. The effect of cyanide was instant. Commandoes forced the hands of the remaining alive suspects to their back and tie them with nylon rope. Commandoes holding their arms make them run down the building quickly, push them into an closed vehicle, which with screeching sound moves away from the scene.

At the same time, bodies of the two suspects, wrapped in sheets, are also placed in another vehicle and taken away. Abhijeet addressing the remaining commandoes says, "Search rooms, collect mobile and one laptop, their arms & ammunition and move fast."

The street lights still continue to remain off. Nobody could even sense that a major anti-terror operation during the last ten minutes has taken place. The guard of the building has already been taken away for investigation. When the street lights were switched on, the area looks as normal with no sign of any vehicle of ATS, which may attract Media's attention.

Abhijeet, sitting on the front seat of his bulletproof ATS operation vehicle, with a sense of relief on his face, pressed wireless system button, "Sir, reaching within 20 minutes along with the objects."

SP Rana says "Great, Chief is also arriving at HO, Bravo!"

Data analysis team members and other operation experts who have been called for emergent task, are already waiting for the mobile sets and lap top to extract all the data for analysis. Images of all the suspects including those of dead suspects are sent across other intelligence agencies to establish their identities. Identity of one suspect who chewed cyanide is confirmed by RAW.

Both the captured suspects are put in separate chambers so that they are not able to interact with each other. Chief and other senior officers sit in a conference room, where they can watch the interrogation proceedings on a wide screen. One of the suspects is brought into the interrogation room, his blindfold is removed and hands are untied.

Abhijeet starts interrogation, "See, you have only one option and that is to co-operate with us. Nobody outside the world knows that you have been arrested. This room is fitted with the latest devices and sensors, which will detect if you lie and we will not give you second chance. If you co-operate with us, I promise, you will survive."

Before starting question, Abhijeet gives half filled steel glass water to the suspect to drink, which he gulp in a single go. "Do you want more, take it" and fill it to the brim this time and let him drink it. Abhijeet watches the changing face expressions on the face of suspect and tries to read what is going on his mind, which is moving like pendulum, Yes or No. The moment, Abhijeet sensed some positivity on his face, he asked him, "Relax, what is your name?".

He looked at Abhijeet, "Sir, if I co-operate with you, would you insure my safety?"

"Yes, certainly we will" Abhijeet says with assertion.

"My name is Shanker, I am from Amjamgarh in UP."

"Go ahead, tell me everything" Abhijeet tapped his fingers on the table.

"I am a commerce graduate. I have been trying for job for the last four years, but could not get any. One day, I was approached by Saleem, who has died by consuming cyanide. He offered me to join their organization with monthly salary of Rs.50,000/- and also gave me money in advance. For the last one year I have been working for them. They taught me how to plant bombs and detonate them."

His statement was being recorded by the hidden cameras for analysis. He tells the names of both the dead and another suspect, who is next to come for interrogation. His half an hour statement is recorded.

Chief sitting in the adjoining room say, "Though he has limited knowledge of the terror network, but whatever information he has passed on will certainly be useful."

Abhijeet pats on the back of Shankar and send him back to the confinement cell.

Now, the next suspect is brought in. This time, Abhijeet doesn't offer him water and straightway tells him "We know, everything about you and the terror network you are working for. Your partner is co-operating with us." But the suspect whose name is Altaf Mohamad seems to be stubborn and does not give any reaction. His body language clearly shows that he is not in a mood to co-operate.

Abhijeet opening drawer of the table, take out one syringe which is already filled with some drug, in single move like a cobra snake he injects the content of the syringe into the body of suspect and gave blow on his mouth. Altaf started bleeding from his mouth, within two minutes he starts to lose the resistance and divulges whatever information he has. Altaf being one of the conspirators gives lots of vital information.

After one hour, Head of Data Compiling section enters the room holding copies of a list on the table he says, "Sir, based on information extracted from Altaf, Shankar, Mobiles and Laptop a list of 14 persons in Mumbai and 8 persons outside Mumbai with their full particulars has been compiled."

At about 3.00 a.m., Chief of ATS makes an emergency call to CM of the State to brief him about the operation and to takes his consent for the arrest of 22 persons, out of which, there is one leading contractor. CM gives his approval to go ahead. ATS teams, fully equipped to meet any eventuality, are already on move to different destinations.

Rana comes on the line and addressing all teams says, "Boys, go ahead with your mission and send feedback of every development."

Control Room, which is monitoring movement of each team with the help of Information Technology.

Abhijeet is given assignment to apprehend a Contractor, because as per the information divulged by Altaf, the culprit is guarded by his musclemen armed with lethal weapons and there is possibility of resistance.

The first arrest is made from Mahim slums where the suspect is nabbed while sleeping after consuming half bottle of liquor. Rana from Control Room says, "Put this suspect in the lock up of Mahim Police Station and move for one more suspect from Dharvi. His address has been sent to you over SMS."

There is shoot out at Malad West, where the ATS team receives resistance from other gang members of the culprit. ATS Commandoes overcome the gang and instead of one they take three persons into custody.

By 5.00 a.m. one after another, Control Room received confirmation from 12 teams. Only teams of Abhijeet and one more DSP, whose targets are far away, are left to confirm.

Abhijeet, on approaching to the location of the object, gets down from the vehicle and moves alone by foot, rest of the team members follow him keeping a distance of 25 metres. Reaching closer to the premises, he could see through his night vision that two persons relaxing on armed chairs in the balcony of first floor, which means the target is on the first floor. There are two cars parked outside the premises of house. Abhijeet over wireless tells his team mates about the plan. One of the commandos silently gets closer to the cars. He sprinkles some explosive power on both the cars, putting them on fire takes shelter behind the wall. Both the cars flare up creating horrifying scene for both the guard. They come down to see what happen. Abhijeet and the Commandoes emerge from behind the wall, in quick move slit open wind pipes of both the guards with sharp commando's knives and move fast towards the house. The contractor, on listening disturbing voices of his guards, also comes out of the house. Abhijeet with a single blow makes him immobilise, by that time ATS vehicle and other team members also arrive, put the contractor into the vehicle and move away. They can hear many shouting voices behind them coming from the house.

By 6.00 a.m. in the morning all 15 shortlisted persons were locked in different chambers pending their interrogation. Control room gets confirmation of arrest for 8 shortlisted persons outside Mumbai. By 7.00 a.m. news of ATS crackdown leaks out to media. At 8.30 a.m., a Spokesperson from Home Ministry addresses a Press Conference briefing media persons about busting of one terror network, who were responsible for number of past terror incidents and were planning nefarious activities in the State of Maharashtra.

ATS Chief expresses his appreciation for the whole team of ATS for successful clinical operation. Abhijeet gets applause from all the seniors and his colleagues and he feels elated, at least he is able to make some beginning. He is looking for more excited operation with full of action. He is the Hero of the Day. Abhijeet, first time, experiences a strange feeling of satisfaction for achieving something appreciable. Such achievements remain embedded in the memory, oozing pleasure to oneself for a very long time to come, perhaps for rest of your life. He gets motivation for more and bigger achievements.

For the next two days, all the shortlisted 23 persons in custody are grilled one by one. Voluminous information and data is extracted from them. Based on the information, more operations are conducted to find out the key operators of the terror network.

Abhijeet and other Officers assemble in the conference room to discuss the outcome of the interrogations conducted with the arrested suspects. Analysts, who have analysed, after watching the interrogations of each suspect, gives a sensational news that four of the suspects have mentioned about links with Somalia, which needs further investigation. Excerpts from the interrogation videos are displayed on the screen. Everyone in the conference room agrees that there is some strong link of Somalia with the terror network. It is decided to interrogate these four suspects asking Somalia specific questions and see if a concrete picture comes out.

Further interrogation of these four suspect reveals that weapons, ammunition, explosive material, electronic devices and money comes from Somalia through drug smugglers, delivered at the remote sea shores. It is the swapping of drugs, which comes from Pakistan, with the arms & ammunition delivered by smugglers. Delivery point can be western Gujarat or Maharashtra sea shore, every time it is different. It means drug money is being used to finance terror activities. The money is distributed amongst all the terror operatives as per the instructions sent along with the baggage. From the call records of the mobiles confiscated from these suspects reveals that they received calls from different countries and every time through different landline phone so that identity of the callers could not be established.

Abhijeet proposes to the Chief of ATS that he himself will go to Somalia, mix up with the local gangs there and find out the key conspirators operating from there. Somalia, being hub for sea pirates, smugglers and other international criminals has become a criminals' paradise. Foreign criminals are allowed, if they are hired by any local pirate or smuggler gangs. His proposal appears to be too risky. Chief and other senior officials gave silent gaze at Abhijeet, how dare devil this young Commando is so confident to carry out such an operation, where the risk factors are too high. Chief, after long silence gives his nod for the proposal says, "OK, I will speak to Chief Minister, but, from now onwards, you will have a code name 'Arjun', a detailed action plan be prepared and submitted to me."

Chief, before leaving the Conference Room shakes hand with Abhijeet and patting on his back says, "I am proud of you my boy."

Abhijeet with a bowing gesture says, "Thank you Sir, for confiding in me, I am honoured".

Chief with a smile on his face leaves the room. All the senior officers, present in the room, one by one shake hands with Abhijeet, wishing him success in his mission. Rana has tears in his eyes and he embracing Abhijeet says, "I am sure, you will create a history in the organization."

A Support Team of five officials, headed by SP Rana is formed for project "Eagle" to prepare a detailed action plan, taking into consideration all possible eventuality. Besides Rana, the team consist of two DSP level officers from Control Room, one Data Analyst and one weapon Expert.

Rana addressing the Support Team says, "Puntland, the Northern State of Somalia, is a Pirates dominated area, where number of such gangs are operative and sometimes they hire foreigner with exceptional criminal records. Any stranger found moving around alone is shot down without any warning. New entrants have to move along with his other gang members till his recognition is established amongst the locals. Most likely, the kingpin of the terror network, is headquartered somewhere in Puntland. We are identifying some leading gang where Abhijeet as a professional killer can be inducted."

With the help of graphic technology, number of changes on Abhijeet's photograph are tried on computer to give him an entirely new look. Ultimately, they zeroed in on an appearance, wherein, he has small hairs, one big scar on his forehead, flat nose is given slight pointed look, colour of eyes is changed to grey to give it a criminal look, eye brows trimmed, moustache are removed. A black mole is created on the right cheek. Even Abhijeet himself in his new look will not recognize himself. In his new avatar, he has to undergo training to learn how to behave like a hardened criminal.

Through plastic surgery scar is created on his forehead which appears to have been caused due to sever injury. Black mole is embedded on his right cheek and shape of his nose is changed. All these activities are done at a secrete lab. His new name is Babu Markande, who belongs to a remote tribal village of Maharashtra. He studies each location of Somalia, its roads, clubs, different gangs their history and after practice of two weeks, he can behave like a criminal. Within the ATS organization it is told that Abhijeet has gone to a friendly country for further training.

Through Mumbai Police, advertisement with sketch of Babu Markande, who is responsible for kidnapping and killing of number of people is published in local and national newspapers. An award of Rs.50,000/- is declared for information leading to his arrest. There are number of murders take place every day in Mumbai. On the advice of ATS, Mumbai Police keeps on holding Babu responsible for many cases and declared him as a serial killer. It is broadcasted on all TV networks and there is lot of criticism of the Police Department for their failure to arrest him. On certain occasions, he appears in public places, making himself conspicuous by carrying gun in his hand and firing shots in the air just to create havoc, but by the time police arrive at the scene, he disappears. There are lot of rumours and stories amongst the underworld about Babu.

ATS team has been waiting for response from an Interpol covert Agent in Somalia, who is tying up arrangements for Babu's induction into an organized pirates gang, whose commander Yusuf Jamal is known to Interpol covert Agent Rustam Mohamed. Jamal, who is an Engineering Graduate from Bangalore, has reputation of six successful hijacking of large ships and about dozen medium size vessels. He has made more than $15 millions through piracy and has started financing of hijacking operation by other pirate cells, whereby minting money without exposing himself and his gang members to the risk of getting killed. Jamal has contacts with the higher authorities as he keeps them on paying role with lucrative sums on regularly.

Rustam has spoken to Jamal regarding induction of Babu, for whom Indian territory has become too hot because he is on the Most Wanted Lists of many agencies. Babu, who was commando in Indian Army, killed fellow soldier over a dispute, deserted Army and turned as a freelance professional killer. Jamal checks antecedents of Babu on Internet and was keen to hire him. Jamal advises Rustam that if Babu can manage to reach Garowe International Airport, from there he will be picked up by his people.

At Garowe Airport, Babu gets down from a turbo plane of Emirates Airlines. There are only two planes of Somalian Airlines parked at the airport. He walks down to the terminal. At the entrance of the terminal a well dress Somalian in his mid-fifties extends his hand for him and says, "Hello Mr. Babu, I am Jamal. You are welcome to Somalia."

"Thanks, Mr. Jamal". Babu has already done lot of study on Jamal at ATS.

Jamal while escorting Babu out of the terminal says, "Do I look like a Pirate? Don't be confused! What we are doing, is all for noble cause to help the poor people of our country. All those civilized people are concerned with their ships, but they have never thought of our people".

When they approach a brand new shining black Toyota Fortuner, one of the two bodyguards, with AK-47 hanging on their shoulders, comes forward to take luggage from Babu and places it on the vehicle from the back door. Another guard opens rear door for them to get in. The driver of the vehicle remains unmoved behind the wheel. One bodyguard sits on the front seat beside the driver and another climbs from the back door and vehicle moves on.

Jamal continues to conversation says, "Babu, you know, I have done my computer Engineering from Bangalore. I like that city." He gets silent for a moment and then again continue "I have seen your history. You are a professional killer by accident. You will have good prospects if you work for us. There is lot of money you can make in a short span of time and then you can live a luxurious life anywhere, say Singapore or Dubai for rest of your life. I know, you have that potential." Jamal puts his hand on Babu's hand in an assuring gesture. Jamal could sense that Babu is more than a harden criminal, because while listening to him his eyes were exploring each and every building, shops, movement of the people. An ordinary criminal cannot possess such characteristics. He has to be careful while dealing with Babu.

Babu is able to sense what is going on in Jamal's mind and immediately reacts, "What did you say? Tell me again. Actually, I was wondering around the streets."

Jamal feeling relief, "It is OK, we will talk on the drink, you may be tired".

Babu laughs and says, "No way, I never get tired. I am a working machine."

Toyota stops in front of a villa for the gates to be opened by a guard. Abhijeet could read the name plate inscribing "Yusuf Jamal" affixed at the main gate. There are many villas in this locality, which must be a VIP area. When they get down, Jamal directing to one of the Guards says, "Take the luggage to the Guest Room on second floor."

Both, Jamal and Abhijeet walk towards a glass doors, which automatically slide open when they approach to enter the house. There is a spacious lobby with a fountain in the middle. Two stairs in curve shape, made of Italian marble, lead to the first floor are on both the side. There is one lift also available for going to second floor.

Jaml says, "Babu, you can change and come down after half an hour we will meet for lunch. Guard will escort you to your room."

Babu finds there are CCTV cameras at Gate, Lobby and even in the lift. The guest room is much bigger than a normal size room of any hotel. Babu thinks, *They must have screened my baggage before placing it in the room. Jamal is an extremely conscious person with exceptional understanding and he will be watching my every movement.*

There is a large dining table, big enough to accomodate twelve persons. Jamal and his wife Fatima are already sitting when Babu joins them. Jamal introducing his wife to Babu says, "Meet my wife Fatima".

Fatima shakes hand with Babu and says, "How are you Babu? Jamal told me about you. We really appreciate people who can deliver result. Have seat!"

"Thanks Madam."

Jamal, putting salad in his plate, looks at him and says "Babu, as you know we are in a business which entails high stakes. There is lot of international resistance for piracy. Therefore, in the changing scenario, I am diversifying my business to construction, cargo shipping. So far, I have been hijacking ships, but now I will need to protect my ships from pirates."

Jamal takes two spoons of soup and says, "Do you get my point? I need someone who can protect my interests. In Somalia, there is large scope for business of construction because all infrastructure facility have to be created from scratch. It is the right time for me to diversify my activities to areas, where I can flourish with peace of mind."

Babu, who have been listening to Jamal says, "What will be my role in your new enterprises? I am on the run, Indian police hunting for me, sooner or later, they will trace me out and ask your government for my extradition. I can't expose myself to people."

Jamal assuring him says, "I have thought over this aspect in details. With my good contacts at the highest level in the Government there will be no problem. Just relax. I can assure you full protection."

He continue to say, "I have purchased around one thousand acres of land, on the outer skirt of Garowe, where I have plans to create an industrial and residential complexes. Today, I will take you there to show the area. You will be assisting me in all security matters, because our law and order situation will take some more time to stabilize."

After lunch, Babu comes to lobby and sit on sofa kept for waiting. He tries to assess the situation thinking, *It will be rather a better assignment than to be part of the pirate operation. At least, I will not be party to any act which may be termed as a crime as per the local laws. I will be in a better position to proceed in my mission of tracking down and elimination of epicentre of terror network.*

Jamal comes in the lobby and says, "Let us move. It is half an hour drive from here." He hands over one Beretta M9 Pistol along with its belt holster and one extra magazine to Bobu and says, "Keep it with you whenever you go out. It is loaded. Extra rounds are placed in your room's cupboard".

Babu ties the belt of holster to his waist and says, "Thanks, I have used this handgun in number of operations. It is my favourite gadget." Babu positions the gun on his left side. With the possession of M9 semiautomatic pistol which holds 15 bullets of 9 mm in its magazine he can handle any situation.

About 5 kms away from the city, their vehicle enters a premises through an iron gate. There is a temporary construction office constructed. Two heavy dozers and one loader have been deployed for land development. It is an extensive huge land from one end to another end and they have already done barbed wire fencing around the area. Jamal comes out of the vehicle. Acknowledging greetings of the person who comes to receive them, tells him, "Rafeek, tell everybody Babu will be the In-Charge of this project from now onwards."

Addressing Babu he says, "Besides this huge land, I have also purchased limestone mines and land, which are 100 kms away from here, where I plan to put up a large cement plant. There is great demand of cement for construction in Somalia and we don't have many plants to produce enough cement. I am looking for a right partner with experience in cement industry for the same."

Babu looking around the area says, "What is your planning for this land?"

Jamal gesturing his hand towards the land says, "Here, I have big plans for this place. See, after 25 years of turmoil, we do not have any infrastructures, no education system, no industries. Here, I will develop a new modern city and will showcase it to these western countries we can do it. I need your help to fulfil my dream. Will you?"

"Sure, I will! It will be my pleasure to be part of a noble cause, where many homeless people will get homes to live and children get education." Babu is surprised to see and thinks, *How a pirate can have so constructive and positive approach.*

Jamal gets sober and says, "I know, you must be surprised to see a pirate with such welfare plans for the people. I have done piracy all these years to mobilise funds for these causes. I am not a criminal!"

Jamal gestures with hand towards his vehicle and says, "Let us get back before it gets dark. We may have some obstructions on the way."

When their vehicle reaches a turning point, the road is blocked by boulders. The moment vehicle stopes, four gunmen appear behind the bushes. Both the bodyguards in the vehicle try to pull their guns, but Jamal holds them back. Jamal addressing Babu says, "Let us go down and talk to them."

Both of them get down, raising their hands move towards the gunmen, who were training their guns at them. Jamal addressing the gunmen very politely says, "What do you want? Don't you know me?"

One of them says, "We know you very well, but who is this stranger and what is he doing here?"

"He has come here to assist me in my project. Believe me he will not create any problem for you." Jamal says with assuring tone.

"Sorry Jamal, we have instructions from our boss to take him in custody and he will decide on him."

One of them totters Babu with his gun to move towards their vehicle and remaining three persons hanging AK47 on their shoulders move behind him. Babu, after walking for few metres, in a quick move snatches gun from that man and hits hard on his head with the butt of the gun, making him to fall down. Before, other three fellows could react, Babu hit them one by one in a fraction of moment that all lie down on the ground.

Jamal, who was watching all this, claps with both hands and coming closer to Babu says, "Relax Babu, they are all my people. I wanted to see some action from you. You have performed well. I like it. Now let us move."

Entering Villa, Jamal looks at Baha and says, "Get yourself changed, see you after one hour at my bar We will talk more over drinks."

"Definitely." Babu taking two steps with each stride reaches his room for changing his dress.

In the bar, adjoining to the dining hall, both Jamal and Babu sit on high stools near the bar counter. Attendant places two drinking glasses and one bottle of Black Label Johnnie Walker scotch whisky – a favourite brand of Jamal.

Jamal pours whisky in the glasses and putting ice cubes says. "OK, Cheers for our long association!"

Babu also toss the glass and says, "Cheers".

Jamal finishes his glass in a single go and wait for Babu to finish his portion of drink, who also gulps drink in single shot.

Jamal with appreciating tone says, "Good, I like it. You can keep pace with me." He pours more drinks in both the glass. Holding his glass in both the hands, he presses his lips and then looks at Babu says, "Babu, I have told you what I am, what are my future plans and what for I am hiring you." He takes sip from his glass and says, "Babu, now, it is your turn to tell me the truth about you. I want to know your true identity and your actual purpose of coming here. I know that person Rustam, who has introduced you to me, is a covert agent of Interpol. We have been functioning in connivance of each other for mutual gains."

He sip drink and continue to say, "Believe me, I will not harm you and if your purpose is not in conflict with my interest, I will rather like to help you. Take drink, I know, you are type of a person who knows no fear."

Abhijeet maintaining his composure says, "To be honest with you, I can confide in your words. I am a covert Agent of ATS Maharashtra and I am in pursuit of kingpins of a terror network, who are making life difficult for our people. The network is being controlled by their leaders, who are hiding in Somalia. Most probably, they are either Pakistanis or Indians. They are supplying weapons, explosives and money through drugs traffickers for their network in India."

Babu sipped drink before continuing, "Last month, we apprehended more than a dozen persons in different encounters. During interrogations they have revealed about their Somalia link. Now, it is up to you to decide."

Jamal, in a thoughtful manner speaks, "Actually, Rustam did tell me that you are an ATS covert Agent and you were coming here on an important mission, perhaps he is also not fully aware of the whole facts. You see, in our profession, it is only trading of favour. I will definitely assist you to track down your objects, but in return I do expect from you or your people similar gesture. There are numerous ways to do that. Hope, I have made my stand clear."

Babu does not hesitate to respond and says, "In my personal capacity, I owe your favour and would also talk to the higher authorities about your contribution for our mission. India being one of the leading countries of the world in cement manufacturing, we can help you to have joint venture for your proposed cement plant."

Babu can see sparkling in Jamal's eyes and continue to say, "Provided you can get all requisite approvals and assurance from your Federal Government that the interest of Indian Company will be protected."

Jamal with firm voice says, "Our government will welcome any such proposal because creation of infrastructures and development of industries is on top of their agenda. Cement is the most essential raw material for any construction."

Jamal finishes his drink and continue say, "I hope and believe, your government will reciprocate my gesture of co-operation. You need not to disclose your real identity to anyone and continue to remain as a fugitive from India."

They take more rounds of drinks till 10.00 pm, then have dinner and saying good night to each go to their respective rooms.

Babu, though he has consumed lot of liquor, but still he has full control over his senses to prepares a detailed report of the day in coded language and e-mails it through his IPad to SP Rana. Within ten minutes he receives back confirmation to go ahead. Rana also mentions that through Ministry of Industries they will contact Cement Manufacturers Association to find out if anyone is willing to put up a cement plant in joint venture with Jamal.

After two days, Rana intimate Abhijeet that one of the leading Indian cement manufacturers is willing to put up a cement plant in joint venture and they wants to visit the project site and negotiate with Jamal. Babu at lunch time, while sitting at the dining table, says, "Jamal, I have been intimated by my HO in Mumbai that one of Indian Cement Manufacturers is willing to have joint venture with you. They intend to visit project site. They will come by their private plane. Their site visit arrangements and safety measures have to be organized by you."

Jamal with prompt reply says, "Great! When are they planning to come?"

"May be during next week. Their exact programme will be intimated. Better, if you can fix up meetings with the concerned Minister and other Government agency. Just for confidence building."

"It will be done, my dear Babu." Jamal is so excited that he hugs Babu and kisses him on his cheek. His wife Fatima also seems to be happy about this development, because it is going to be turning point in their life. He has been running pirate operations for the last 25 years and all of sudden undergoing transformation as an Industrialist who will be providing employment to thousands of Somalians to earn their livelihood. Jamal settles down over his mobile, giving instructions to various persons. He talks to the concerned Minister for Industrial Development, who confirms to have meeting with the delegation coming from India. Jamal makes arrangement for a helicopter to take the members of Indian delegation directly from airport to the site to show them land and limestone ores. As per the report of the UN survey, the quality of limestone is ideal for commercial manufacturing of cement. There are sufficient reserves of limestones to last for five decades. He makes arrangements for their stay in one of his villas.

Babu while eating rice says, "There will be no mention about me. It has to be kept strictly confidential till we accomplish our mission."

"Don't worry, I can understand. There will be no laps." Jamal assures him.

Babu thinks, *we have moved one step forward, now it is his turn.*

Visit of high level Indian delegation concludes with positive notes. All the available survey reports for the limestone mines, available with the Ministry of Industries, were given to the visitors for preparing project report. It is decided to put up one million tonne per annum capacity cement plant in the first phase. There are possibilities for five million tonne per annum cement product from the limestone reserves, which are sufficient enough to produce cement for fifty years. It has been agreed upon for 50:50 ratio equity participation of both the parties. Indian company will provide technical know-how, plant and machinery and would commission the project. For the initial 2-3 years, Indian company will provide technical experts and supervisory staff. All workers and staff, recruited locally, will be given training at cement plants in India during the construction period free of cost. An MOU is signed between the two parties in presence of Minister of Industries.

Two weeks have passed since Babu landed in Garowe, but most of the time, he is confined to the villa. One night, Jamal takes him to a pub, which is frequented by underworld operatives. A table was already reserved for them. Mustafa, the owner of the pub, is known to Jamal. A sealed bottle of Jamal's favourite whisky is placed on the table along with ice cubes and glasses. A topless waitress serves drinks to both of them.

Jamal says to waitress, "Call Mustafa, I want to speak to him." Waitress bows and leave. After couple of minutes, a fat man with thick moustache holding cigar in one hand comes to their table, greeting Jamal and Babu he sits on a chair opposite to Jamal.

Mustafa taking puff from his cigar says, "Sir, what can I do for you?"

Jamal gulp drinks from his glass and placing it back on the table says, "See Mustafa, I will pay you handsome amount for authentic information regarding a network of smugglers, who are probably Indian or Pakistani. They are mainly engaged in drug business and supply of weapons to a network of terrorists in India. This should remain between you and me, otherwise you know."

A warning from Jamal sends shudder through his spines. Mustafa gathering some confidence says, "Please give me two days and I will come to your residence with complete details." He stop for a moment and remembering something says, "A group of three Indians with one Pakistani do come here once in a fortnight. Their sittings last for 3-4 hrs, discussing something in their language."

Jamal finishes his drinks, pours more drink and gulp it again and says, "Find out all details about them and whenever they comes next time, make recording of their discussion and also inform me."

Mustafa recollecting about their last visit to his pub says, "Wait, they came here about ten days back and their images must be available on CCTV camera records."

"OK, just now, go through your CCTV recording, when you are able to locate them, we will come to your computer room to see."

Mustafa gets up and moves holding his cigar in his fingers. Jamal turns to Babu and say, "This man is scared shit and he will get me full details then we will decide our further strategy."

Babu with smile on his face says, "We have to move fast and with umost care to reach them before they get alarmed. Their network is very strong. By now, they must have learned about my presence in Garowe."

When the both are having drinks and eating mutton kabab, which is a speciality of the pub, a persons with bald head, wearing specks, in his late thirties, comes to their table and say, "May I joint you? I want to speak with Babu."

Babu raising his eyebrows says, "How do you know me?"

That man pulling one chair, says, "My name is Ahmed Patel and I belong to Baruch district of Gujarat. I am running containers service in the port city of Bosaso."

Taking out his visiting card from his wallet, he places it in front of Babu and continue to say, "I know your reputation through my people in Mumbai. You are on the most wanted list of many Indian agencies. I have an assignment for you worth more than a million Rupee."

Babu showing no interest in offer says, "See, I am already hired by Mr. Jamal to look after his interests. He has very high ambitious plans. I am not available."

Patel, now addressing Jamal says, "If you don't mind Mr. Jamal, can I also have a drink?"

Jamal pouring drink for him say, "Sure, it's our pleasure to meet you. By the way, what assignment do you have for Babu, which carries such a high premium?"

Patel taking a sip of the drink, "See, more the risk, greater the prize. If you associate with me, it will be for our mutual benefit. We can have our long term relationship."

Babu looking in his eyes says, "Who is the target you intend to liquidate?"

Patel leans forward to get closer and says, "Two Officers of ATS Maharashtra, one is DSP Abhijeet and another SP Rana, here are their photographs." He takes out one envelope from his pocket and hands it over to Babu.

Babu, without taking out the photographs from the envelope, gets the glimpse of the photos of Rana and of his own. Babu takes few sips from his drink and say, "Why do you want to hit them, any specific reasons?"

Patel hesitates and says, "See, I am running underworld activities in Mumbai involving stakes worth millions of Rupees, but lately these ATS cops are making difficult for our show to run. I have already lost half of my network there. Before mobilizing my team again I want to remove these obstacles. I will give you one million in advance and balance one million of Rupees after the job is over. Both of you are welcome to visit my office tomorrow evening at Bosaso. We can finalize the deal. I will be waiting for your call."

Addressing Jamal, he says, "Thanks for your drink. I know you are a man of great reputation. I have seen news about your proposed Cement Plant. You are a dynamic person. I am glad to meet you." He shakes hand with both of them and leave.

After he left, Mustafa gets closer and says, "He was one of them."

Jamal retorts, "OK, now we know him, what about identity of other three persons."

Mustafa, with a requesting tone say, "Would you mind to come with me?"

Both, holding their glass of drinks follow him to an adjoining room, where Mustafa displays clippings of videos on a monitor. At one point Jamal says, "Hold display here and enlarge the face of the person who is wearing white salwar."

Jamal recognizing the man says, "I know him, his name is Abdul Rehman. He is a drug trafficker. Mustafa find out where does this man live?"

Mustafa with beam on his face say, "Sir, I know lot of drug traffickers, who come here regularly. It will not be difficult to locate him. Give me just ten minutes. You may please go back to your table and have food." Mustafa gets busy with his mobile talking to his contacts.

Babu taking his seat, prepare fresh drinks says, "We are pretty close to our destination."

Jamal taking a piece of kabab with fork says, 'Once we catch hold of this Abdul, he will spill the beans."

Mustafa comes back holding a piece of paper with an address written on it. Handing over the paper to Jamal and sasys, "Abdul lives at the outer skirt of the city in a slum. At the moment, he is in his room after taking dose of drug and can be picked up without any resistance. If you wish I can send one of my boy, who happens to come from the same locality, along with your team to locate him."

Jamal makes call to his aide and explains him how to carry out the operation without coming to the notice of anybody and bring the object to the place where such persons are interrogated and sometimes tortured to death.

Jamal's face getting red, says, "Babu, now it is time for action. We have to move fast before Patel gets alarmed. After 20 minutes a black vehicle arrives with dark glasses on the windows. One young man of 26 years gets down from the front seat and walks in the pub. Getting close to the table of Jamal he says, "Yes Boss."

Mustafa also comes with one of his waiters. Jamal pointing to the boy says, "Listen go with them and never open your mouth. Now move fast." By now, except Babu & Jamal nobody else is there because it's already 1.00 a.m. of night. Babu and Jamal also get up to move. Before leaving pub, Jamal takes out a wad of money from his pocket and gives it to Mustafa, "Keep it Mustafa. Make sure your boy keeps mum."

Mustafa putting wad of the money in his pocket says, "I have already warned the boy to not to tell anybody about all this otherwise he will face horrible consequence."

Jamal and Babu sit in the Toyota Fortuner and return to the villa. After half an hour Jamal receives call from his team leader saying, "Sir, the object is in our possession. He is down with heavy dose of drugs, hence no use of questioning him till he gets to senses. Taking him to the stores."

Jamal says, "Well done, we will come by 10.00 in the morning."

Next morning, while taking breakfast and on way to the location where Abdul has been detained. Babu observes that Jamal does not speak even a single word except saying good morning. He gets silent when it comes to an operation. When they enter a room where Abdul is tied to a wooden chair, Jamal extends his hand towards the young man who came to the pub last night. His name is John, a professional killer, working for Jamal for the last 15 years and his close confidant. John takes out one large commando's knife from the drawer of the table, kept along the wall, and hand it over to Jamal.

Jamal blandishing the razor edge sharp knife towards Abdul says, "If you don't co-operate and answer our questions, you will be beheaded and I mean it."

Abdul, who is so scared manage to say, "I know you Sir, I have nothing to do with you."

Babu intervenes and says, "But you have a lot to do with me. I am DSP Abhijeet from ATS Maharashtra".

Abdul gets so scared because he has heard a lot about him and his nervous system breaks down, making his salwar wet. Abdul in a shaking voice says, "It is only Patel, who is responsible for all that being done in India. I am in the business of co-ordinating drugs from Pakistan through my contacts. I am limited to this much only."

Babu, who has disclosed his real identity of Abhijeet, says, "We are short of time, answer our question properly, no lying and no hiding."

Abhijeet getting closer to Abdul asking him, "Give us complete details of Patel's actual activities. For which terror outfit he works and who are the other key persons in Somalia? Answer quickly." Jamal gets to the other side of Abdul.

Abdul realising if he wants to survive, he has to tell them everything, says, "Ahmed Patel is the head of the terror arm of IS for India. He receives funds and arms from them. All the stuff comes through containers of his own company. There are number of containers filled with arms and ammunition lying at Bosaso port. I can identify those containers. There are three more Indians involved in these activities. They also operate from his office. Details of his network in India are available on his computer." Abdul stops for few moments and then continue to say, "I know, this much only."

Jamal taking John away from there says, "Give him food and if he tries to escape or communicate with anybody, kill him. We are taking him to Bosaso port. You along with five more commandos with full preparation come in separate vehicle following our vehicle. Bring Abdul along with you. Will start from villa within one hour."

Jamal and Abhijeet both select weapons of their choice from the armoury in the villa. Both put on bulletproof under their shirts. Before leaving Jamal speaks to Chief of Police over phone and explain him about the containers full of weapons, which may be used for creating trouble in Somalia. Police Chief assures him full support from Bosaso Police force.

Jamal and Abhijeet both enter their vehicle and move for Bosaso. John along with his team and Abdul in another vehicle follows them. All of them have come prepared for action. They are hard core fighters and have taken part in many such operations in the past. After five hours non-stop journey they reach port city of Bosaso. Jamal owns one villa in Bosaso also, which he occasionally use whenever he visits the city. Jamal decide to take food and some rest at villa before going for the action.

From villa he makes phone call to Patel and says, "Hello Mr. Patel, its Jamal this side. Babu and I both are in your city to take forward our last night meeting and would like to give final shape to the plan. What about that five star hotel on the beach."

Patel being a conscious person never go for a meeting at a venue suggested by other party and says over phone, "It will be nice, you both come to my port office at 9.00 pm, where my other partners will also be available. We will discuss our future plans thread bare while having few rounds of drinks. I will be waiting for you."

"OK, we will be there sharp at 9.00 p.m."

Jamal calls John and briefing him further action says, "Look John, you know the port area well. Note down address of the office where we are going to have meeting to take action. You reach there by 8.30, park your vehicle around there under shadow unnoticed. On receiving my signal, your team will enter the building, search for classified documents, and removing hard discs from all computers. Since the police will also be raiding that place too after short while, you must finish your job before their arrival, go back to your vehicle and get out of that area."

John says, "Sir, what about Abdul".

"Lock him in the basement of villa, put one guard over there. We will hand him over to the police later on."

At 8.15 Jamal says to Abhijeet, "Abhijeet, I hope you will not mind if now I call you by your real name.

Abhijeet with smile says, "But avoid before Patel for some more time."

"I will. What about having a drink before action."

"No problem." Abhijeet moves towards the bar to fetch the bottle of drinks.

Jamal received confirmation from John about their reaching at the location. It is 8.35 and will take 20 minutes to reach there. Abhijeet realizes, despite taking heavy peg of drink, Jamal has become silent, perhaps he is mentally preparing himself for the action. Abhijeet has already sent message to Rana about his proposed action. At ATS control room, all senior bosses are waiting for the final outcome of the action.

When they reach at Patel's Office complex, before entering a guard tries to frisk them, but Patel himself comes to the reception to receive them and says, "You are welcome to my office" and shake hands with both of them. The guard moves back without frisking them, otherwise any weapon is supposed to be deposited at the reception itself.

Patel escorts them to the first floor through steps. His office is very well designed and nobody can imagine about its being used for organizing terror activities in another continent.

He says, "I will show you my office." His office is a spacious room, with luxurious sofas lined up for the guests. He has installed all sort of latest communication system to have video conference. There is a big curve shape table with luxurious chairs, which Jamal has not seen anywhere in Somali. Patel, open one of the cupboard behind his chair, takes out one bag, lock back the cupboard and puts the keys in his pocket. Abhijeet makes it out that all important papers must be placed in the cupboard that is why Patel keeps the keys in his pocket.

Patel placing the bag in front of Abhujeet says, "First thing first. Here is the advance money. If you don't mind. I would like to introduce you with my other partners. They are in the conference room. If you like my office, we can continue to have meeting here itself."

Abhijeet gesturing his hands says, "It's a wonderful room and quite comfortable."

Patel calls his office boy and says, "Inform others sitting in the conference room that meeting will take place in my office. They may come here. Bring drinks and snacks for all."

After few moments, three Indians enter the office. They shake hands with both of them one by one introducing themselves. Abhijeet realizes that they are not giving their real identity and were introducing themselves with fake names. Suddenly, it struck to his mind that he has seen photo of one of them from the criminal records of the terrorist. That man also become conscious and gets up, goes closer to Patel and whispers something in his ears. Abhijeet could clearly read from the face of Patel what is going on there. Jamal also sense that something has gone wrong. May be the man is able to make out that Babu is some covert agent of ATS and something suspicious has definitely happened.

Abhijeet watches Patel's right hand lowering down may be to pull out a gun or to press some alarm button. Jamal also sends signal to John.

Within few moments, five gunmen appears behind them holding their silencer fitted automatic guns, one of them shouts at Jamal and Abhijeet and says, "Raise their hands."

Abhijeet while turning back to see what happened, pulls his M9 pistol and shoot down all the five gunmen instantly. While Patel and his other accomplices try to run away, Jamal shoot them one by one. At the same time, John and his team also arrives and they start search operation. Abhijeet takes out keys from the pocket of Patel to open that cupboard where important documents were being kept. He quickly put them in one bag and also takes out one laptop from the cupboaerd. He collects mobiles of all the key persons.

Abhijeet, Jamal and other team members move out of the building. While going back to villa, Abhijeet sends message to ATS "Mission Accomplished".

Jamal informed Police Head about the incident. Within half an hour, a senior Police Officers with force comes to villa to take away Abdul Ahmed to identify the containers which are filled with weapons. Next morning all the newspapers and television channels are covered with news of having captured huge quantity of weapons from the terrorists.

Next morning Jamal and his team along with Abhijeet return to Garowe. Next day evening, Jamal and wife Fatima come with Abhijeet to Airport to see him off. Abhijeet checks in two big suitcases full of documents, laptop and mobile so as to generate work for data processing section of ATS. He takes sound sleep in the plane. At Mumbai Sahara Airport one Airhostess wakes him up saying, "Sir, we have arrived at Mumbai airport." Abhijeet looks around to find that all passengers have already boarded down.

When he steps down, Rana comes out of ATS vehicle, which is parked near the plane and says, "Welcome back Abhijeet."

Abhijeet shaking hand with him says, "I have two black colour suitcases with yellow ribbons tied on the handles to be picked up from the luggage. Here is my boarding pass to confirm luggage number."

Rana giving boarding pass to one of his assistant and say, "Collect these suitcases and bring them to office."

Abhijeet is taken out of the airport from a different channel because he cannot be exposed in the public till he regains his original appearance of Abhijeet because Babu is still on the most wanted list of Police. Character of Babu will be remembered as a covert agent in the history of ATS.

When they reach ATS Head Office, Abhijeet is given red carpet welcome by the Chief and other senior officials.

As soon as the two suitcases are received, segregation and processing of all documents, mobiles and laptop, hard discs is taken up by the Data Processing wing. Abhijeet once again undergoes plastic surgeries for removal of scare from his forehead and giving his face same original shape, which takes almost a week time. After that he is allowed one week vacation to visit his family at native place, which he has been missing for a long time.

CHAPTER - III

Sub-Inspector Vaishali, who is one of the best lady Police Officers of Maharashtra Police force, is transferred to ATS and attached to Abhijeet. She is a tall with broad shoulders, boy-cut hair style, wears no earrings or bangles and walks like a lioness. She knocks door of Abhijeet's Cabin. Abhijeet, who is busy studying file of recent smuggling cases, without raising head says, "Yes, come in."

Vaishali saluting Abhijeet says, "My name is Sub-Inspector Vaishali reporting for duty to work under you, Sir." She exerts emphasis on her last word in a typical forces manner.

Abhijeet raising head says, "Welcome Vaishali. I have heard lot of praise about your dare devil performance. Come have sit."

He closes file and put it aside. "So, what does make you to get transferred to field operation job of ATS? It is too a tough job for a lady. Of course, you have proven record of outstanding performance. Anyhow, would you like a cup of tea?"

"No thanks Sir, I just had it in HR Section." She removes her Mumbai Police Officer's cap and places it on the table. ATS uniform is yet to be issued to her.

She looks at Abhijeet with admiring says, "Sir, you are a legendary commando. I feel myself lucky to be associated with you. It will be great learning and thrilling experience to work with you."

"Thanks Vaishali. You can go to your seat and get acquainted with your other colleagues."

Vaishali, coming out of the cabin she thinks, *Fucks, what a charming guy he is. He is a type of person I have dreamt of throughout my life. One day, I am definitely going to marry him. Hope, he is not too fussy. Let me see.*

Sub-Inspector, Mahesh, who happens to be her colleagues earlier, introduces her to other colleagues and explains her about the working systems. Vaishali, who has been listening to all this, says, "Hey, you guys why are you so tense, it looks like a class room. What's the matter?"

Mahesh in a suppressed voice says, "Listen, Abhijeet Sir is very strict. No fun. Only work and results. So, be careful!"

Vaishali in a defiant tone says, "Fucks, I have my own fucking way of working. Take no tension. Focus when you are on the job in the field and then no kidding."

Mahesh says, "Vaishali, you will never change. I missed you a lot during these period and now I am happy to work with you again. We will have good time together."

"Mahesh, no more flirting with me. I had told you in the past many time. I have a different image of my life partner."

"Vaishali, see, God wishes us to be together, that is why you have been transferred to ATS to work in the same office with me. Don't go against the wishes of the God."

"Shut up Mahesh!"

All personnel in the office like her lively attitude. The whole day, she keeps on moving from one table to another table, keeps on cutting jokes and laughs lavishly. Abhijeet knows, she will become a different person when it comes to action, that is why he does not objects to her and let her do whatever she wants. She is also aware of her limit. Her father is a Head Constable in Police Force and her elder brother is an Inspector of Police.

After two weeks, at about 4.00 p.m., Abhijeet calls in Mahesh in the Conference room, where a meeting with other senior officers is going on, says, 'Mahesh tell everybody not to leave and they should get fully prepared for action. They will get briefing sharp at 8.00 p.m. and we will push off by 8.30 p.m. for long journey. Everybody should have meal before 8.00 p.m.

Vaishali is excited to exercise her killing instinct for the first time with ATS. Everybody observe her getting silent and transforming to into a different personality, her look and body language is changed. She takes double the quantity of ammunition than other members on an average carry. Everybody carries bulletproof and night vision since the operation is to be conducted during night about 150 kms south of Mumbai in the rain forests adjoining to sea shores.

Ram Vinayak

During briefing Abhijeet addressing the team consisting of 24 commandoes says, "We have received confirmed lead that big hauls of weapons, ammunition and explosives will be delivered through launch boats at the sea shore covered by rain forests."

Pointing to a location on the map displayed on a digital screen, he says, "This is the delivery point, where the consignment is usually unloaded from the boats in the shadows of trees in darkness so as to avoid being seen by coastal guards in the second half of the night. After taking delivery of the consignment they disappear in the thick rain forests and the stuff is carried for more than 2 kms on the back of labours, who are paid hefty sum, to reach the road where it is loaded on the trucks and taken away. The launch boats will be reaching between 2.00 to 2.30 a.m. We will reach at this location of the road by our vehicles by 11.30 p.m. From there, we will walk through jungle without being observed with the help of our night vision to reach the sea shore and take position at the location. We will remain in touch with each other through wireless communication system using headphone. Use night vision and laser sight attached to your guns. Try to capture as many alive, but no one should escape."

Looking at Vaishali he says, "It is your first operation, better you remain besides me and don't underestimate your objects. They are hard core terrorists." Concluding briefing he says, "Any question? OK let us move."

Vaishali sits beside Abhijeet in the leading vehicle, followed by four more vehicles. She was silent like Jamal used to be. Abhijeet knows such persons becomes lethal weapon and killing machine when it comes to action. At 11.45 p.m. they reach a location from where they have to go by foot. Vehicles are hidden behind the trees with one commando along with driver remaining inside each vehicle with the guns loaded to meet any eventuality.

While moving through thick jungle, Abhijeet was in constant touch with the Control Room where Rana and other Officers are sitting and watching their movement through GPS. Whenever, there is any fallen tree on the way, Abhijeet holds Vaishali's hand to help her cross the obstacle. Though she can manage to walk over the obstacles, but she prefer to take his help. She likes to grip his hand. Within 40 minutes of walks they reach the location.

Abhijeet makes a call over his mobile to someone to know his location, a torch light flashes twice at a distance of 100 metres. In response Abhijeet also flashes light twice from his pencil torch. Within few minutes a person approaching Abhijeet says, "Salam Sir, there are still two more hours. Boats will come over there on right side about 100 metres from here. More than a dozen labour sitting behind the trees, smoking heroin. Sir, I will also be one of the labour to carry boxes. I may also get trapped in the cross fires."

Abhijeet assuring him says, "You don't come to pick up the load and remain behind the tree, pretending that you have problem in the feet and would not be able to walk with the load. OK, now go."

After one hour, one of the Commandoes, left behind the vehicles, comes on wireless and says, "Sir, one car with four persons besides driver and three closed vans have come and parked about 100 metres ahead of us. Only four persons with AK47 rifles hanging on their shoulders have gone into the jungle leaving behind three vehicle and car."

Abhijeet giving instructions to him says, "When you get message from me or hear gun shots take the occupants of the vehicles in your custody and don't let anyone escape, shoot them if any resistance. Got it?"

Commando says, "Yes Sir."

Abhijeet addressing all commandoes through wires says, "Take position behind the trees on the right side and keep on watching through your night vision. No movement. They may also be having night vision, so be careful to remain unnoticed."

At 1.30 a.m., Abhijeet through night vision spots four persons appearing from the trees. Now, they are holding their rifles in a fighting mode. From walking style, Abhijeet makes out that they are definitely professionals. One of them climbs on a rock and through his night vision start to scan the surrounding area and then comes down and using his mobile talk to somebody. More than a dozen persons, who are labourers hired to carry the loads, appear behind the trees and they all sit near the shore.

At distance, deep in the sea, there is continuous flash of light. The man standing on the rock flashes light from a hand held flash light. Three high speed large boats appear getting closer to the shore. Abhijeet addressing to Commandoes who are carrying automatic grenade launcher rifles says, "Don't let the boats get away shoot them when action starts."

"OK Sir," two voices comes on the wireless.

Rana from Control Room comes over wireless and says, "Abhijeet, Coastal Guards have been alerted to capture the boats, however, you are at liberty to take your decision, if you want to destroy them, you are free to do so."

"Sir, if Coastal Guards will shoot them on high seas, there will be hue and cry on the media for boats being fishing boats. I will finish them here only so there is no ambiguity left for anyone to give any twist to terror incident."

"OK, go ahead Abhijeet, you are behind the wheel."

Three persons came down from boats, they shake hands with their counter parts on the shore, and the labour start to download boxes from the boats. When Abhijeet feels, most of the boxes have been down loaded, addressing all commandoes says, "Aiming with your laser sights, run and fire. Fire grenades."

With the sudden volleys of gun shots terrorists and persons from boat start to collapse at the spot. Each boat is hit by 2 to 3 high powerful grenades and start burning and suddenly all boats get into splinters with the explosion of the explosives which are still left on the boats with the flash lights and deafening explosions the whole jungle get lit up and birds start creating noises.

One of the four terrorists is seen running towards the jungle. Before Abhijeet could give any instruction for him, Vaishali starts running to catch hold of him. Abhijeet also run following her. He don't want to take any chance, because she has come first time for the action. To his great surprise, Vaishali reaches terrorist before he could get lost in the rain forest. She hits him on the back making him to fall on the ground and then putting her gun on his head says, "Don't move you son of bitch. I will shoot you." When he tries to move, she hits his head with the butt of her gun and making him unconscious.

Abhijeet, who is standing near her says, "Relax Vaishali, well done, at least we are able to catch one alive." Other commandoes handcuff the terrorist and pull him from there.

Commandoes waiting in the vehicles also get to action to apprehend all the vehicles along with their occupants.

Abhijeet and Vaishali walk down to the dump of boxes unloaded from the boats. Remains of the burning boats also sink in the water. Abhijeet taking round of the boxes, says, "Open this large box carefully."

One of the Commandos with his commando's knife opens the box, looking with his torch light says, "Sir, it M24 American Snipper Rifle."

"Put the lid back to close it." Abhijeet addressing to Control Room says, "Sir, operation is over. Should we move back with stuff?"

Rana coming on the line says, "Wait for some time. Coastal Guards boats are reaching you within few minutes.

You can hand over the stuff to them. Police force is already on way and would reach you within an hour to take custody of dead bodies and the labourers involved in these operation. But bring that price catch, which you are able to apprehend alive for interrogation. Search those dead bodies and collect their mobiles for data analysis. That's all."

Abhijeet tells one of commandoes to collect mobiles of the dead terrorists. Abhijeet addressing Commandoes in the vehicle says, "Police force is reaching you any moment. Hand over those culprits and four vehicle to them."

Three Coastal Guards boats arrives with force. They lit the area with their search lights placed on their boats. Their senior officers comes to Abhijeet and shaking hand with him says, "Sir, myself Commander Mukherjee. Congratulations for this successful operation."

"Thanks Commander. Now, it's all yours, we got to move now."

"Sir, you need not to go back through jungle all the way. My boat will drop you at a point from where you can take your vehicle."

Abhijeet with gesture says, "Well, that's wonderful idea!"

Abhijeet addressing his team members in the vehicle says, "When you have handed over the vehicles and their occupants, come back to the point where road hits the sea shore, we are reaching there by Coastal Guards' boat."

All commandoes with the arrested terrorists board the boat, which moves with lightning speed on water and within few minutes they reaches that points from where they are to be picked by their vehicles.

By the time, they reach Head Office, its morning time and Vaishali falls asleep resting her head on Abhijeet shoulder. He is an ardent believer in professional ethics, hence for him she is another colleague and her gender does not matter for him. On reaching Head Office, she get up and says, "Sorry Sir."

"It's OK Vaishali. Your action in those moments is adorable. You have passed your first test with distinction marks."

"Thanks Sir."

Abhijeet along with his team goes to the Conference Room, where Rana congratulated every member one by one and says, "Boys, the Department is proud of you. You can go home and relax for the day. In the evening I am arranging a cocktail party for you."

All of them, before leaving, say in one voice, "Thanks Sir."

Rana coming to Abhijeet says, "We will handle your price catch after few hour. Let us go to the Rest Room and relax for couple of hours."

In Interrogation Room, Abhijeet places three photographs to the captive and says, "You have already witnessed to what extent we can go. Now co-operate and answer my questions. If you lie, I will cut your fingers and ears to begin with without delays." He stops for moment and continue, "What is your name and which place you belong to?

"My name is Aslam Khan from Sholapur."

"You are working for which organization and for what purposes consignments of these weapons have been sent and by whom?"

"These are sent by Lashkar-e-Toiba from Karachi for killing VIPs and political leaders."

"Where do you live in Mumbai and your other colleagues were killed last night?"

"We all live in a house in Thane and there we have a warehouse, where these weapons were to be stored. These weapons were to be given to the sleeper agents on instruction from Karachi. We don't know who these sleeper agents are."

"Besides four of you, who else are the people in India working for your network?"

"I do not know anybody else. My other colleagues, who are dead, used to talk over mobile with them."

Abhijeet before concluding interrogation say, "An ATS team will take you to Thane to search your home and the warehouse, where you are hiding weapons and explosives."

Rana talking to Police Commissioner of Mumbai Police over phone says, "Sir, role of Makbool Ahmed, owner of the captured vehicles, needs to be examined thoroughly. We need to find out his financing sources for procurement of ten new vehicles, which he has procured during the last two months. If it is terror money, it means he is a bigger player. Let CBI complete their investigation, but they need to take up matter on top priority."

Police Commissioner with assurance says, "I will tell CBI commissioner to coordinate with you and expedite the matter."

"Thanks Sir." Placing the phone on cradle Rana says, "Abhijeet, don't you think, Makbool may be a key person?"

"Definitely Sir, there are number of calls made by him to those three dead terrorists. He is certainly a major link. We can yield details of sleeper agents out of him. I fear, CBI may mess it up. They should let us handle Makbool."

Rana connects to the CBI Commissioner and says, "Good morning Sir, SP Rana from ATS."

"Yes Rana, I was just now speaking to the Police Commissioner regarding Makbool. Our team with Makbool will be reaching you within an hour to hand him over to you because I feel you are in a better position to handle this man. Hope, you will agree with this arrangement. What do you say?"

Rana with prompt reply says, "It will be nice because he is the missing link for us to proceed. Thanks for your consideration Sir." And phone gets disconnected.

In the interrogation room, Abhijeet says, "Look Makbool, we know you are part of this terror network, rather a major operator. You have been making calls and coordinating with them on regular basis which is confirmed from call records of your mobile. Some of your accomplices have been killed in an encounter, but there are lot many sleeper agents and you know their details."

Abhijeet before coming to the point offers him a cigarette and lights it from his lighter, says "We can have deal. The deal is, you give us details of the sleeper agents and become approver, we will let you off with minor punishment so that you can go back to your family and continue with your business. You have only two options, either accept our offer or subject yourself to unbearable sufferings and spend rest of your life behind the bars. Now, the choice is yours."

Makbool takes deep puffs from the cigarette till it exhausts. Throwing cigarette butt in the dustbin he says, "What is the guarantee?"

Abhijeet in an assertive manner says, "I am a competent authority. If we will not honour our words, nobody will cooperate with us in future. We don't have personal enmity with you. Our purpose is to safeguard citizen of this city. Your wife and nine children also live in this city. You are a sensible person. Rest assured, not only you will be let off we will provide you security. Here is your mobile, take out their name and contact numbers and also tell me their addresses one by one." Abhijeet takes out a note pad from the drawer and starts noting down the details one by one. When it is over, he pats back of Makbool and says, "Relax Makbool.

For the time being you will remain with us and later on we will send you to a safer place."

Abhijeet goes to Control Room, where Rana and other officers were watching the whole proceeding on a big screen. Rana with smile on his face says, "Well done Abhijeet! How conveniently and tactfully you have handled him. Now, the whole terror network of Lashkar-e-Toiba in Mumbai stands busted. Abhijeet, I have no words of praise for you. You are a genius possessing rare combination of brain and brawn."

Next morning Rana calls Abhijeet to his chamber and says, "Abhijeet, while interrogating one of the sleeper agents, who happens to be from Karachi itself, it is surfaced that one retired Brigadier of Pakistani Army, Rahmat Malik is the kingpin behind this network." Rana placing pointer on a location on the digital screen says, "This is the farm house on the outer skirt of Karachi, which is being used to store explosives and weapons in the basement of the house. The house is guarded round the clock by retired army soldiers. Drug trafficking and arms supply is the main profession of the Brigadier Malik. Arms are mostly smuggled through Afghanistan boarder. He supplies weapons for a price to any terror outfit whether it operates within Pakistan or in India. His only concern is money. Pakistani intelligence agencies have gone so corrupt that they ignore his activities because all concerned officials have their cut on his illicit transactions. He maintains good rapport with all political leaders too." After taking break for a while he continues to say, "Capturing of his weapons and destruction of his boats by ATS must have given him big financial jolt and if we continue to foil his future attempts to smuggle weapon into Indian territory, he will become bank corrupt. He is keeping his most of the money in Swiss Banks. Since this money is being used for terror activities, through Interpol we are trying to seize his Swiss Bank accounts. RAW has confirmed that now a days Malik is in Bern, the capital of Switzerland."

Abhijeet, who has been listening to Rana, says "At this point of time, we can go and liquidate him there."

Rana says, "In view of our relationship with Swiss Government, I don't think it will be possible. However, we can supply evidences of his involvement in terror activities in third countries to Interpol and Swiss Authorities."

Abhijeet says, "Sir, at present, since Malik is in Switzerland, any covert agent can meet him over there as an IS activist and for carrying out IS activities would finalize deal with him for the supply of weapons by paying him advance money. I am sure, he will take the bait. At that moment, Swiss Intelligence Agency can arrest him. Once he is in their custody for terror activities, we can extradite him from there for the terror activities carried out by him and the Government of Pakistan will also not come to his rescue."

Rana conceding to the idea of Abhijeet says, "That's great idea Abhijeet. Abhijeet, let me talk to the Chief and explain him the details, if he allows, we both will go to Switzerland to discuss the matter with Strategic Intelligence Service. Better you get prepared and collect all relevant facts about Rahmat Malik."

Contacting Chief over Intercom Rana says, "Sir, Rana this side. For some important matter can I meet you?"

"Sure, you can come just now."

After half an hour, Rana comes back with smile on his face and says, "Chief has Okayed our plan. He is speaking to Swiss authority about our visit."

Rana giving instructions to his lady secretary says, "Reena, arrange reservation for Abhijeet and me for Bern by tonight flight and send flight details to Chief' PS, who is coordinating for our transportation and hotel arrangement there."

Addressing Abhijeet he says, "Hope, by evening two sets of dozier will be ready. Carry soft copy of the same also."

After 12 hours of journey, when the plane lands at Bern Airport, it is early morning and chilling cold out there. An intelligence officers of Swiss Intelligence Service escorts them to a vehicle to take them to Hotel. He straightway take them to the room which is already reserved for them and says, "Gentlemen, you can take rest for couple of hours. I will back by 10.00 a.m. to take you to the Head Quarter. Your meeting is scheduled at 11.00 a.m."

There are more than ten senior officers of Swiss Intelligence Service present in the conference room. Mr. Joseph their Strategic Head addressing to Rana says, "Mr. Rana, your object is under continuance surveillance of our Field Operation Agents. He is certainly a dubious character.

The dozier submitted by you makes it a matter of concern for our security. We can't allow such fugitives to move around in our country. Any terror incident will have adverse effect our tourism industry."

Joseph takes break for few seconds and continue to say, "As per the plan proposed by you, one of our Agents, disguising himself as IS activist will meet Brig. Malik tonight in Coffee Bar of the Hotel, where he is staying, and try to strike a deal with him for the supply of weapons at double the prevailing price. Once the bargain is recorded, we will apprehend him at the spot. Dozier given by you will come in handy to frame charges against him."

Rana says, "Can you arrange to seize his bank accounts in Swiss Bank?"

"Unless we arrest him, we can't notify banks to seize his accounts, but we are keeping watch on his transactions."

At the Coffee Bar of the hotel, where the meeting of Brig. Malik with the covert agent, four tables have been wired and covered by CCTV cameras so that audio and visual recording can be done simultaneously. Intelligence Service agents have placed "Reserved" plates on these tables to ensured that none of these tables are occupied by anybody. As soon as Brig. Malik enters Coffee Bar these plates are removed from the tables by the Agent who is standing there wearing waiter's uniform. Malik comes and occupies one of the tables. After the gap of ten minutes, one person enters bar, looking around the bar, he comes to the table of Malik and says, "Mr. Malik?"

"Yes, please take seat and tell me what do you want?"

"Myself Ezaz Ahmed. I am Member of Great Caliphate Movement. We are committed to promote Islam in this country. In our bid to take forward our Jihad, we have mobilized funds. We are in need of some sophisticated equipment like sniper rifles, hand guns with laser sight and silencer, high explosive devices, night visions and many more items. We have long list of items. We can have a long term business relationship for this noble cause. We have abundance of funds. Price will be yours."

Malik finds a prospective customers in a country where he feels the authorities are not fussy. He takes sip of black coffee from his coffee mug and says, "See Ezaz, it involves lots of expenses to bring stuff from Pakistan to Switzerland and there is lot of risk too. I can arrange to deliver any sophisticated weapons or devices at Karachi Port, will arrange custom clearance for the consignment, get it loaded on the ship and my responsibility will be over."

"No problem. We will let you know the name of the European port where the consignment is to be sent. Rest we can managed."

"One thing more, I will take 100% amount in advance in cash."

"No Problem, to begin with please arrange small consignment of ten hand guns of latest model with silencers and ten thousand rounds of cartridges. How much it will comes to?"

Malik calculate the cost on his mobile and says, "It will comes to US $110,000, however as gesture of our first deal, I will take US $100,000".

Ezaz placing one brief case on the table, flap open it showing the content of the same and says, "Here is an amount of US $200,000, half of the amount is for this deal and remaining you keep with you to be adjusted against our next deal." Closing the brief case he tosses it towards Malik.

Malik grabs briefcase by its handle and stand up and says, "Here is my business card. You can contact me over mobile. Don't send details on e-mail. Khuda Hafiz!" Holding briefcase he turns to move, but finds himself surrounded by sleuths of Intelligence Service and two Officers of ATS. He gets so scared that the briefcase drops from his hand and he collapses on the chair. Looking at the face of Ezaz, he says, "Who the hell are you?"

Ezaz, without giving any response, walks away from there. Two Intelligence Officers handcuff Malik and push him into a vehicle along with the briefcase and move away.

Joseph shaking hands with Rana and Abhijeet says, "Your idea has worked. Now, this bastard is going spend rest of his life behind the bar."

Next day, Mr. Joseph addressing a Press Conference says. "A retired Brigadier Rahmat Malik, who has been involved in number of terror activities, has been arrested. He has been found promoting terror activities in our country. Here is video of the deal he has made with our covert agent for the supply of weapons, which itself speaks of his involvement in terror activities in our country."

On returning to India, Rana and Abhijeet get busy to prepare documents for extradition of Malik from Swiss authorities to India. Malik has caused the greatest embarrassment to the people and Government of Pakistan.

CHAPTER - IV

Addressing an emergency meeting of the officers Rana says, "RAW has confirmed information of a terrorist outfit having planned to disrupt the final ceremony of Ganapati Visarjan when thousands of people gather at various sea sores to participate in the function, but the location of their attack is not confirmed. They may create havoc at multiple targets. Any suicidal attack may lead to stampedes making situation worst. Only three days i.e. 72 hours from now, are left and we are clueless. Come what may, we have to stop it. How do you do it, do it? We have to prevent any untoward incidents. Chief Minister is very much concerned about it."

There is pin drop silence for some moments. Then Abhijeet says, "We have to start exploring from whatever sources are available with us. We may start with that Makbool Ahmed, a transporter who turned approver in case of weapon smuggling. He may be in a position to give us some lead. I would also like to go through the list of terrorists apprehended in the recent past. We may get some lead from any one of them. All informers must be told that there will be handsome incentives for reliable lead."

Without wasting any moments, everyone leaves conference room to make calls and they start leaving office for different destinations in search of some clues about the terror attacks. Abhijeet, sitting alone in the conference room, go through the profiles of terrorists who are in custody and also those who are still at large. He shortlist five terrorists, who are yet to be nabbed and can be expected to be involved in the terror attacks feared to be happened after three days. Handing over profiles of these shortlisted terrorists to Control Room Abhijeet says, "Forward these profiles to Police Head Quarter, all police stations in Mumbai and all check posts with clear instruction that these are most wanted terrorists by ATS. Strict watch need to be exercised at all railways station, bus stops and public places for the next three days."

Abhijeet goes to the cell of Aslam Khan, who was apprehended during one of the operation and is undergoing trials for his terror activities. Abhijeet entering the cell and says, "Aslam Khan, I have a deal for you, which can earn you acquittal from all charges, if you are able to assist us in nabbing terrorists who are planning to create problems after three days on the occasion of Ganapati Visarjan ceremony."

It takes Aslam Khan with surprise and he says, "Sir, I will definite avail this opportunities, if luck favours me I may be able to find out who are these people." He thinks for few moments and then says, "Sir, I know one person, his name is Umar Quraishi, living in slums of Andheri East. He keeps himself update with any underworld activities and sells information for a price according to the type of information. That area is inhabited by criminals and usually unfamiliar faces are not acceptable there. If I will come along with you, there will not be any problem because they knows me well. Nobody else should come with us, otherwise it will create unnecessary alarm. For an outsider, It is something like going into hell. You have to carry good amount of money, because in such dealings there are no negotiations."

Abhijeet goes back to the office of the Jailer to speak to him and then send two constable to bring out Aslam from the special cell of the jail. When Aslam is brought out, his handcuff are removed and Abhijeet says, "Let us move first to my office, where I will change my uniform and collect money."

Aslam sits beside him and vehicle moves from there. After many days, Aslam is able to see the outside world.

When they reach Andheri East area of slums, vehicle is parked outside the slums and from there Abhijeet and Aslam walk through zigzag narrow lanes of slums. Abhijeet finds it stinking like rotten rats all around due to trashes littered everywhere. An airbag, filled with money, hanging on his shoulder and handgun under his shirt, Abhijeet keeps on walking fearlessly as if he belong to this place only. He finds there are number of houses which are being used by the prostitutes, whose business, even at late hours of the night, is still going on.

On reaching a double storey house, Aslam knocks the doors. After few moments, a voice comes from inside, "who is there?"

"Umar Bhai, I am Aslam just released from the jail."

The doors open and a middle age person peeps from the gap of the door saying, "Who is along with you?"

"He is friend of mine. We have big deal of business for you, may be worth anything."

"OK, get inside."

Umar stares at Abhijeet and says, "Now tell me, what do you want?"

Abhijeet flip opens the bag and shows him the money and says, "Look I mean business. For the right piece of information, I will pay you more than your expectation, but don't ask us question."

Umar gets slightly scared with the firm gesture of Abhijeet and says, "OK, what do you want to know?"

"On the occasion of Ganapati Visarjan some terrorist are planning to create problems. Who they are and where we can find them?" Abhijeet can make out from the body language of Umar that he has the information, but hesitating to answer. Abhijeet pulls out his gun fitted with silencer and placing it on his head says, "See you have two option either give me information and take money or take bullet through your head. Now, choice is yours."

"OK, I will tell. Two days back, five persons from Azamgarh, UP have come to Ganesh Nagar in Malad. One of my friends, Zhaheer, who runs Taxi service, has taken them round the beaches where the Ganapati Visarjan ceremony will take place. Zhaheer has told me that they are going to create big trouble, may be some explosions. In fact, Zhaheer wanted to inform Police Station at Malvani, but I told him not to do it, he will unnecessarily put himself in troubles. Since you have come with money and I work for money."

Abhijeet get up and says, "Keep this bag with you and take us to Zhaheer immediately."

Abhijeet, Aslam and Umar walk out of the slums to take their vehicle, parked over there. While on way from Andheri East to Malad West, where Ganesh Nagar is located, Abhijeet calls Rana and says, "Good news Sir, I have located objects. Already on way to Malad West. Please send ten commandoes to Malvani Police station. They should wait for me over there."

"Great, I will manage it and would be available in Control Room. Good luck Abhijeet!"

Reaching near the locality, where Zhaheer lives, the vehicle is parked and all the three walks down to his house. Zhaheer willingly comes with them to show the house from where he picked up those five persons.

Abhijeet along with Zhaheer and other commandoes of ATS moves to Ganesh Nagar. On reaching the location, Abhijeet addressing Commandoes says, "Try to capture them alive. If anybody resist or try to escape shoot him. Blow open the doors and catch hold of those bastards."

Two commandoes with the single blow of their kicks blow open the doors and all commandoes with the torch lights attached to their guns enter the different rooms in the house. Six persons sleeping in three rooms get up grabbing their guns. Abhijeet shouts at them and says, "Don't move. Throw your weapons down." Two terrorists try to fight back but commandoes' bullets penetrate their foreheads before they can raise their guns. Remaining four are taken away by the commandoes. In the meanwhile Police force also arrive at the location to take possession of dead bodies, explosives and weapons from the house.

Rana from Control Room comes on line and says, "Well done Abhijeet in less than 24 hours you have apprehended the culprits, who could have caused havoc to the people of Mumbai.

The apprehended terrorist tell during their interrogation that they were planning to plant explosives in the vehicles which will be carrying idols of Ganapati at various locations of Mumbai and detonate them to inflict maximum loss of life and leading to stampedes. One of the two who died in ATS encounter was their contact in Mumbai.

After this successful operation, Aslam is let off with minor punishment by ATS. Zhaheer Taxi Driver is gifted with new Taxi by the State Government. Umar is directed to work as Informer for ATS and remain in touch with Abhijeet.

CHAPTER - V

It is the evening time of Tuesday, at 7.30 p.m., two trains arrive at Andheri (East) railway station. Thousands of commuters get down from both the train and throng of people returning from their working places, comes out through the exit of Railway Station. As usual, they move out in hurry to either catch autos or run for a BEST buses to reach their homes. All of sudden, bursts of bullets start hitting them from different directions, which continue for more than two minutes. Hundreds of commuters screaming with the ensuing pain of bullets piercing through their bodies run amuck and subsequently fall down. People on the front try to go back, but could not resist the pressure of the commuters coming out and fall down and get crushed in the stampede. After committing massacre at Andheri East railway station, all the four perpetrators run away from the scene and board a white Bolero to vanish away.

Within minutes, deafening sirens of ambulances and police vehicles makes the scene of carnage worst for the already scared commuters who have not yet come out of the shock. Many of them are so shaken that they are unable to move. Station and platform is scattered with broken mobiles, shoes, chapels and lunch boxes. The exist point area, where the shoot out took place, is smudge with blood. Dead and injured are being taken away by ambulances and other vehicles. Police have cordon off the area. A team of ATS under Abhijeet is busy collecting the empty shells of AK47 rifles which have been used by terrorists.

White colour Bolero Van is located parked on the roadside 4 kms. away from the railway station. A team of forensic experts takes out finger prints from the van, which was stolen two days back from Thane, but the registration number plate has been changed. As per one of the witness, who has seen five persons coming down from the van with one big bag, which must be containing AK47 riles used for the carnage of innocent commuters, tells ATS team that they switched over to another vehicle already parked there and moved away. As per the witness, it was Swift DZire of white colour and the number plates end with 3945.

Rana coming on the line from Control Room says, "Abhijeet, a white colour Swift DZire has been seen going towards Thane and one of the finger prints taken from the Bolero Van match with finger print of one Raju Patel, who was recently released from Pune jail after a term of four years for drug trafficking."

Abhijeet says, "Sir, please contact Pune jail to find out with whom this Raju Patel used to interact in the jail and he should be brought to ATS office for interrogation."

"OK Abhijeet, you can carry on with work there and keep me inform. Raju's inmates will be here before tomorrow morning. I have already alerted Thane police to locate Swift DZire with 3945 number plate."

After half an hour Rana again comes on line and says, "Abhijeet, that vehicle is located in Majiwada of Thane."

Abhijeet after thinking for few moments says, "Sir, tell thane police to find out from property dealers, who deals for Majiwada location, if they have stuck deal for any outsider in that area during last fortnight or so. I am moving with my team to Thane."

"Great, you have almost hit the target. I will revert back soon. I am sending one more team from here to Thane."

After half an hour, when Abhijeet with his team is heading for Thane, Rana comes on line and says, "Abhijeet, one Mohan Palekar, who deals in properties of Majiwada area is detained in the Majiwada Police Station."

"I will reach there in another forty minutes. Please ask ATS team team to reach at Majiwada Police Station."

Mohan Palekar, who is in his mid-thirties, gets scared to see ATS team. Abhijeet in an assuring tone says, "Relax Mohan, we will not hurt you. Tell me full details."

Mohan gathering some courage says, "Sir, about ten days back a person may be around 28 years of age, who appeared to be from Gujarat, came to me for taking a flat on rent. He readily accepted to pay a rent of Rs.35,000/- per month plus security and my commission of Rs.35,000/- all in cash. He did not even negotiate. He was carrying one suitcase only and nothing else. When I asked him about his luggage, he told me it will come after a week time. His name is Sadiki Mohamad. I have the copy of the agreement signed with him."

Abhijeet spreading the map of Majiwada on the table, says, "Show me the house on the map."

Mohan putting his finger on the map says, "Sir, this is the flat on second floor."

Abhijeet studying the location on map says, "Ok, Mohan you go and sit in another room, but don't leave the police station." By now, another team of Commandoes has also arrived. He calls in all the commandoes and pointing to location on the map says, "In front of the house, there is wide road and on the back there is service lane. It is 11.30 p.m. now. After one hour, we will start operation. Four commandoes with Inspector Shinde move right now and keep watch on the house with night vision. It is a two bed rooms set. Since they don't have any beds, at least six persons must be sleeping on the floor. They are armed with deadly weapons. Everybody should wear bulletproof."

Abhijeet addressing Vaishali says, "Vaishali it is a close encounter, you can stay back."
"No Sir, I am coming with you."
"OK, be careful."

Abhijeet addressing to Police Station In Charge says, "At 00.30 hrs, please stop traffic on this road from both side. Nobody should be there on the road in vicinity of the house."

"It will be done Sir."

Inspector Shinde comes on the wireless and says, "Sir, on second floor at the window, there is one person sitting on the chair with AK47 on his lap, keeping watch outside the road. It is not possible to enter the house without being watched."

"No problem Shinde, in that case, we will stop vehicles in front of the house and assault second floor through staircase. Before that man in the window could make alarm, you can get him by snipper rifle shot with the help of night vision."

"OK Sir, I am taking position."

Sharp at 00.30 hrs, when three vehicles of ATS stop in front of the house and commandoes in black uniforms rush in the building, the person sitting at windows receive bullet in head, but with the shattering sound of the window glass alerts the remaining terrorists. Abhijeet knows it is going to be fierce battle, but there is no other option.

Two commandoes with the blow of their kicks open the door. Abhijeet fires with his hand gun at two terrorists in the drawing room. Vaishali following him enters the room with her hand gun pointing to different directions. All of sudden two terrorists comes out of a room and fires burst of bullets at her. Before Abhijeet could take them, one of the terrorist has already fired all the 30 rounds from his AK47 all hitting on her chest. Other commandoes liquidate the remaining one terrorist of the second bed room.

Though she was wearing bullet proof, the impact of 30 bullets fired so closely from AK47 have caused too much damage to her lungs. She is unable to breathe and falls down. Abhijeet hold her hand says, "Vaishali, don't worry you will be OK."

She clinches his hand and try to say, "Sir, I love…..". Her hand loses grip and slam down. She vomit blood and her head drops to one side, with eyes staring open.

Abhijeet checking her pulse, closes her eyes with his palm and says, "Call ambulance to take her body. She is no more."

Next day, her body is cremated with full police honour. Abhijeet, seeing Sub-Inspector Mahesh sobbing at the cremation ground thinks, *Perhaps, Vaishali wanted to tell me that she loves Mahesh.* Abhijeet will never know whom she had actually loved!

CHAPTER - VI

Rana calls an emergency meeting of his officers in the Conference Room and says, "There is bad news! As per the information of Intelligence Bureau, about 5 kgs of nuclear waste has been brought in the city by some terror group. Their intention is to prepare a dirty bomb and with single strike expose thousands of people to deadly radioactivity spreading cancer disease and panic, which may cause unmanageable exodus of population from the city. We don't know where the hell this stuff is being kept, whether they have already made the dirty bomb and what is their target? It can cause mass destruction."

There is a pin drop silence in the conference room. Rana continue to say, "With every passing moment, we are running short of time. We have to find out the dirty bomb, before it is too late to avoid the holocaust. Today, we are facing an ultimate challenge to save the city. Use your professional capability to the hilt. This information should not be leaked, otherwise people will become panicky and it will make our task difficult."

Abhijeet, who has been listening in a pensive mood, says, "Sir, as per my knowledge, the nuclear waste has to be stored in a special type of container, which has multi-layers of different material to prevent radiation. These containers are manufactured by only few companies in the world. Standard container size is to carry 200 ltrs of nuclear waste. They must have carried this stuff in some ordinary container and courier might not have been aware of the its content. There are all possibilities that the courier and the person who is safeguarding the container must have received enough radioactivity exposure to develop cancer. Even the people living in the vicinity of the place where this stuff is being kept, might have developed cancer. We have to check with each cancer treatment centre and clinic if they have received any such cancer patient, who, in their opinion, might be the case of radioactivity exposure. If we can spot even a single such case then rest will be routine task."

Rana, who has been listening to Abhijeet attentively, says, "I agree with your views. Let us distribute areas to each one of our team to conduct this survey. I am available in the Control Room round the clock. Abhijeet, you will co-ordinate this operation. Data section will provide you list of all centres and clinics where cancer patients are being treated. Now, you can go ahead."

Next day, by evening, one of the ATS officials, Inspector Kanetkar intimating Control Room says, "Sir, I have just now been told by the Doctor of the cancer clinic being run an NGO in Kalyan West that during the last three days they have received abnormal cases of more than half dozen patience with early stage of cancer. All the patients are from the same locality and two patients of one family. As per the version of the Doctor, these patients might have been exposed to ratio activities. I have taken addresses of the patients. Waiting for your further instructions, Sir."

Rana comes on the line and says, "Well done Inspector Kanetkar. Do not get closer to that area from where cancer patients have come, just keep watch from a safe distance to avoid radioactivity exposure. We are arranging a team of experts from Bhaba Atomic Research Centre (BARC) to handle the material. Abhijeet with his team will reach you in couple of hours."

"OK Sir,"

By evening, a team of Experts from BARC arrives at the location in Kalyan. They put on special protection suits covering all parts of their body and one similar suit is worn by Abhijeet also. They start searching operation with radiation detectors and within few minutes they zero in on a house, wherein the nuclear waste is being stored.

Abhijeet holding his hand gun enters the house. He finds a man lying on the bed unmoved and lots of electronic items are spread on a big table along with other materials used for making bombs. When he opens doors of a steel cupboard, he finds a steel box, usually used for keeping cash. He calls in the nuclear experts, who confirms that the steel box must be containing the nuclear waste. Another specilized container is brought in the room by the team of BARC. The steel box is placed in the container and taken out of the room to place it in a special van, which immediately takes it away from there.

The persons, lying in the room in half dead condition, is taken away by an ambulance to cancer treatment centre.

All people, living in the neighbourhood of the house, are advised to have themselves checked up at Cancer Detection Centre.

Abhijeet feel relaxed having averted a major mishap. Contacting SP Rana over wireless he says, "Sir, operation completed and the stuff carried away by BARC people. House has been sealed for forensic investigation. One man found in the house is in a hopeless conditions due to continuous exposure to radioactivity. His name is Radhey Shayam. Main perpetrators are still at large. Very soon, I will find them out."

Rana feeling relaxed says, "Chief commends your performance."
"Please convey my thanks to Hon'ble Chief."

Same night, Rana addressing operation teams in the conference room says, "Though we have been able to avoid the present crises, but the main perpetrators are moving around in the city and may be planning their next terror activity. Forensic analysis report will be available by tomorrow morning."

Abhijeet, interrupting Rana says, "Sir, we have recovered copy of consignment note from the room of one Green Transport. It shows a wooden box containing a locker despatched from Barmer district of Rajasthan bordering Pakistan. The name of the consignee is Radhey Shyam. It means, nuclear waste has been smuggled from Pakistan. Barmer being a smaller place people knows each other and it is easy to find out the consigner who has despatched nuclear waste. I can take morning flight to Jodhpur. It is hardly four hour drive from Jodhpur to Barmer."

Rana Says, "I will co-ordinate with ATS Rajasthan to provide you all assistance. In the meantime, they will find out the Green Transport and the transporter should be made available for enquiry."

At Jodhpur Airport, a senior officer of ATS Rajasthan receives Abhijeet and says, "Hello DSP Abhijeet, myself DSP Tiwari. We have heard a lot about you. There is no match for you in any ATS teams of the country. It is a great pleasure to be associated with a legendary Commando of your stature."

"Thanks DSP Tiwari. What is next?"

"Let us go to our branch office, where we are holding the transporter, who is ready to co-operate with us."

Abhijeet placing consignment note of Green Transport before the transporter says, "Tell me everything about this consignment. Who did book this consignment? Has he booked similar consignments for other cities also and where to find him?"

Transporter, who is scared, says, "Sir, one Ramesh who lives in the border village of Munabao. Every time, he despatch different types of consignment, packed in wooden boxes."

"Tell me about Ramesh. What is his real business?"

"I don't know about his real profession."

Abhijeet sensing that the transporter is lying gives a hard blow on his face making him bleed from mouth and says, "You are lying. Tell me what are his business activities?"

"Sir, Ramesh smuggles many items through Pakistan border and despatch them to different places through our transport. Mostly he smuggle weapons and drugs. This time, he sent one steel locker packed in a wooden box. We charge him exorbitant prices for his consignments."

Addressing DSP Tiwari Abhijeet says, "Let us move for Munabao. Take this man also along."

On reaching Munabao, transporter shows the house of Ramesh. Abhijeet briefing commandoes says, "Surround the house from all side. Nobody should escape. I will enter the house first and you can follow me."

Entering the house, Abhijeet finds three persons sitting in the courtyard and smoking hookah. Abhijeet giving them warning says, "Nobody moves and raise your hand."

One of them tries to pull his gun, but before his hand could reach it, a bullet from hand gun of Abhijeet penetrates his head making him collapse on the spot. Ramesh and his colleague are taken to the ATS van.

During interrogation Ramesh says, "I do not know anybody in Mumbai, but I have over heard the person, who brings material from Pakistan side, talking to some

Liyakat Ali. I think, Ali must be running some hotel because Pakistani also mentioned during his conversation with him that he would definitely come to his hotel to enjoy the food. Beyond this, I don't know anything."

Abhijeet before leaving for Mumbai contacts Rana and say, "Sir, there is one Liyakat Ali, who is running hotel in Mumbai. He may please be located. I am reaching Mumbai by 8.00 p.m."

"OK I will send vehicle to pick you from the airport. In the meanwhile we will find out whereabouts of this man in Mumbai."

Addressing Field Operation officers in the conference room, Rana says, "Liyakat Ali runs a Beer Bar in Dharavi area. It is a two story restaurant. The bar is frequented by criminals, where members of different gangs settle their deals across the tables. It appears that his business interests are not limited to beer bar only because the huge sum of money, which he has invested in real estate during the last six months, can't be generated through a beer bar. We have to put surveillance on him to find out who are his other accomplices."

Two days after the beginning of the surveillance on Ali's beer bar, during the late night when bar timings are over, ATS Control Room receives message that four persons from a van have gone inside the bar while the bar staff have already left. Within half an hour Abhijeet along with his team of commandoes also reaches the location. Abhijeet briefing commandoes says, "See we are not going to assault the bar instead we will wait for them to come out."

After wait of one hour at 2.30 hrs, Liyakat Ali along with his four accomplices comes out of the beer bar. Abhijeet and his team of commandoes, in swift move grab all of them, tying their hands behind, push them into the vehicles and move away.

During interrogations, Liyakat Ali admitted his being the master mind behind making a dirty bomb, and says, "I am a sleeper agent for Lashkar-e-Toiba. I was doing this on their instructions. Due to my limited knowledge about nuclear waste, the plan failed because the person Radhey Shayam who was hired to assemble the bomb got too much radioactivity exposure and ATS was able to trace out the location."

CHAPTER - VII

It is morning time of 9.30 a.m., bus stands are crowded with office goers. There are number of commuters, ladies and gents, waiting for the buses for their respective destinations at the bus stand opposite to Infinity Shopping Mall. A crowded bus halts at the bus stand. About 5-6 commuters get down from the front exit gate of the bus and about dozen climb the bus in less than half a minute. Bus moves on towards Inorbit Mall. One middle aged lady, who is left behind is upset and cursing the bus driver for not taking her. Bus has hardly moved 100 metres, there is big explosion in the bus. The impact of the explosion is so powerful that the roof of the bus is torn apart and the bus catches fire. Window glasses of the nearby buildings are shattered with the impact of sound wave created by explosion. Parts of bodies of commuters are scattered all around the area. There is panic everywhere on the road. People run amuck hitting each other.

After couple of minutes, people gather courage and get closer to the bus to see if there is any person still alive. They are enable to rescue anybody because bus is covered with flames. There is no possibility for survival of anyone. The terror attack has caused colossal damage taking toll of more than fifty innocent citizens.

The area of incident is cordon off by the police. Abhijeet along with his team has also arrived. Abhijeet walks down to the bus stand where the bus stopped last time. Addressing members of his team, he says, "There is one CCTV camera at this bus stand. Get me footage of recording when this bus stopped here. I want to see who boarded down from the bus. There must be some witnesses also when bus came here. Take their statement." He continue to say, "I want footage from all CCTV cameras installed at all those bus stands where this stops to pick up commuters."

Abhijeet sitting in his office repeatedly watches footages of video recordings of CCTV installed at different bus stands of that ill-fated bus, which has been blown by the terrorists. He is confidant of getting some clues out of these footages. With keen observation, he watches every commuters boarding on and boarding down that bus. While watching CCTV recording of Mith Square, he finds a middle aged man wearing black pants and blue T-Shirt holding an airbag climbs the bus and at the next bus stop opposite Infinity Mall, while getting down the bus, he is not holding any bag. That man in black pants crosses the Link Road and goes opposite side of the road towards Infinity Mall. After 30 seconds when bus has hardly moved for 100 metres, explosion takes places.

In the conference room where Rana and other officers are present, Abhijeet, displaying that footage on a large screen from Mith Square to Infinity Mall says, "You can see this man in blue colour T-shirt and wearing black pants is holding one airbag in his left hand climbs that bus at Mith Square and gets down here on the next bus stop opposite

Infinity Mall, but the airbag is not there. See, he is crossing the road hurriedly so as to reach a safer place before the explosion takes place. Within 30 seconds of his leaving the bus the a powerful explosion took place, killing all commuters on the bus instantly. The forensic report shows that the type of high potency explosive with sophisticated device has been used. Such type of explosives and devices have not been used by any terror outfits so far in any terror attack in the city."

There is pin drop silence in the conference room. Abhijeet continue to says, "The device was either fixed with the timer or might have been detonated by remote control by that man, who after crossing the road and going towards Infinity Mall. With such a high explosion in the vicinity of the mall, it was natural, there was panic in the Infinity Shopping Mall. He manages to enter the shopping through basement entrance into the shopping mall. He, perhaps, forget that there are CCTV camera installed everywhere. He take lift to reach food court on the third floor, goes to a table where a lady is already sitting and eating burger. Sitting at the table he takes mobile from that lady and dial a cell number. Most likely that number is not already saved on her mobile. He speaks to someone may be confirming completion of work. After magnifying the video and running it on ultra-slow speed, we have been able to make out the number he dialled from his mobile. It's a mobile number of Delhi registered in the name of Mubarak Ali. From the call record of Mubarak Ali, it has been found that the call was made from the mobile of Reshma. It means the name of this lady sitting in the mall is Reshma. We have find out her address. She lives in Mahim."

Now everybody in the conference room feel relaxed. Abhijeet continue to say, "Gentlemen Officers, now we have identities of two objects, one in Delhi and another in Mahim, Mumbai. Lady Officers should accompany the team to apprehend Reshma. Before her arrest, we must catch hold of this Mubarak Ali with the help of ATS Delhi, otherwise immediately on arrest of Reshma he will get alarmed. I am leaving for Delhi by evening flight. In the mean while, a surveillance should be done on Reshma. There are possibility of that man who carried out the bomb plantation on the bus, may meet her again. In that eventuality, we can take him too."

While Abhijeet is sitting with Rana, they receive call from Inspector Kanetkar, who is doing surveillance on Reshma, says, "Sir, we have located Reshma's house. The name of that man, who carried out the explosion, is Akhtar and runs he runs an auto rickshaw. Both are husband and wife."

Abhijeet in a dismay says, "Oh shit, it shows Reshma is a house wife and does not appear to be involved in this. Akhtar seems to be some sleeper agent. Of course, he will go to gallows for killing of innocent people, but we won't be able to extract much information from him. Now, we have to apprehend Mubarak to reach the actual perpetrators and their terror network."

Rana says, "Relax Abhijeet, sooner or later, we will find them out."

By 8.15 p.m., plane lands at Delhi Airport. A team of ATS Delhi, headed by DSP Raghav meets him at the apron itself. Raghav shaking hand with Abhijeet says, "Hello DSP Abhijeet, myself Raghav. I am glad to meet you."

Abhijeet reciprocating him says, "Me too. I hope, you must have find out whereabouts of Mubarak."

"Yes, we have located him. He runs scrap business in Mayapuri area. Even after the market is closed, he confines himself along with his other accomplices in the office at his scrapyard. Our two personnel are keeping surveillance on him round the clock. If you wish, we can straightway go from here to Mayapuri and nab him there."

"Yes, we can't wait. He may be planning for another terror attack, may be in Delhi itself. Let us take action, before it is too late."

Raghav, while leaving the airport along with Abhijeet, calls his HO and says, "Sir, we are moving for Mayapuri to nab our object. An additional team may reach there within half an hour and meet us at Mayapuri Police Station."

On way to Mayapuri, Raghav briefing about Mubarak says, "Mubark is one of the leading scrap dealer of Mayapuri scrap market. Iron and steel scrap he dumps in the open yard and scraped electronic items are stored in a small warehouse. He purchases old obsolete equipment and machinery from Punjab & Haryana. He get them dismantled at his scrapyard and supply different items to different industries. It is very profitable business. They make money out of junks. It is suspected, he must be doing smuggling of explosives and devices along with the scrap machines. Every day, hundreds of truck loads come in and go out of Mayapuri market. There is no list of items being carried away from this market. There is always only mention of scrap. It is very convenient to send explosive with devices in any truck load and there will be no check up by any police team on any highways or roads because the scrap is simply dumped into a truck body."

Abhijeet says, "So this is the modus operandi of this terror network. We have to find out the nucleus of this network. It may be Mubarak or somebody else. Once he is nabbed, we have to thoroughly search his warehouse and office for any explosive devices."

Raghav says, "Sure, I will get it done. An ATS team must have reached Mayapuri Police Station."

"Take Police Station In Charge along because he may be acquainted with the area."

At the Mayapuri Police Station, Raghav briefing his team says, "Scrapyard of Mubarak is about 300 metres from here. It is now 11.30 p.m. and there are not many people around. We are going to raid his place and apprehend him along with his one accomplice who is sitting with him in his office."

Raghav addressing to Police In Charge says, "I have just now received picture of the man who is sitting with Mubarak at the moment. Do you recognize this man. He came there by Honda City."

Police Station In Charge, Inspector Shrivastava seeing the picture of the man on Raghav's mobile says, "Yes, we know him. His name is Manvir Singh, an Electronic Engineer, running an industry to assemble electronic appliances by importing parts from China and other places. His factory is located in the Mayapuri Industrial Area itself."

Abhijeet reacting to this says, "Oh my God, surround his factory immediately. Raghav, you will get all that stuff, we are looking far, from the factory of Manvir. You go to that factory with your team and police force available here. Search the factory, stores, office thoroughly and take into custody the workers or Supervisors working in the factory. I will handle Mubarak and Manvir. Inspector Shrivastava you come with me to show the scrapyard."

"OK Sir,"

When Abhijeet and Shrivastava reach the scrapyard, the ATS Agent, who was on surveillance duty also join them and lead them to the Mubarak office. All of them pull out their guns before raid. Abhijeet opening the doors says, "Hands up, don't move or you will be shot dead. I am DSP Abhijeet from ATS Mumbai."

Mubarak, who was drinking whisky, the half-filled glass drops from hand and faces of both turn pale because they know ATS means ringing of death bell for them. Both of them surrender without any resistance. Inspector Shrivastava handcuff them. Abhijeet tells the ATS Agent to collect their mobiles and laptop and seal the premises for further investigations.

Abhijeet, interrogating Manvir at interrogation Cell of ATS Mumbai says, "Manvir, we have found lots of evidences from your factory which establish that the explosive device used in the terror attack was assembled by you. You are responsible for death of numerous innocent people. You are an Engineer by profession running a factory in the prime location. Now tell me why have you done this and for whom?"

Manvir does not resist and says, "I never wanted to indulge in such act, but my business was not doing well and I was under heavy debts. Being a gold medallist engineer, assembling of explosive device was never a difficult task for me. I have all facilities in my factory to do so. Mubarak was aware of my financial constraints. He proposed me to assemble explosive devices, powerful enough to blow and tear apart a bus or train's compartment. For each device I was offered Rs.1 crore, which was quite lucrative sum for me. Mubarak smuggled high explosives from Pakistan through Punjab boarder. I used to assemble the devices during night time when nobody is there in the factory. We could arranged to assemble two devices and in return received Rs.2 crore in cash."

Abhijeet says, "Whom did you send those devices?"

"These two devices packed in company's boxes were despatched to Mumbai to one Sarfaraz Khan running a car garage in Kandivili."

"How is Mubarak involved?"

"He is contact person, who directly gets instructions from terror network operators in Pakistan. Money routed through him. We have received further order of assembling two more devices and we were planning for the same when you raided us."

Rana, who is watching the interrogation proceedings, instantly send a team of commandoes to apprehend Sarfaraz and search his garage and house to recover the explosive device, which has not yet been used.

Within two hours, Sarfaraz was produced in the interrogation cell of ATS and the explosive devices was carried away by the bomb disposal team.

Abhijeet asking straightway question to Sarfaraz says, "Where do you plan to use this device?"

Sarfaraz with hesitation says, "It was planned to use both the devices at the same time on same day. One device was delivered to Akhtar near Mith Square, whereas for another device which was to be delivered to one Yaseen, who did not turn up to take delivery because he got Dengue fever on the previous night. As per the instructions from Karachi, plan for next attack has been postponed."

"Who give you instructions from Karachi?"

"I don't know, calls are received on my mobile, but there is no ID number display. Money gets transferred to my account every month."

"Where is Yaseen now?"

"He is admitted in Municipal Hospital of Andheri East."

Abhijeet thinks, *There may be many more sleeper agents like Yaseen and Akhtar in Mumbai. It is blessings in disguise - many lives are saved due to Yaseen's Dengue fever.*

CHAPTER - VIII

Rana, addressing ATS officers in a tense mood says, "Gentlemen Officers, as per the information of Intelligence Bureau, a professional contract killer has been hired to target some VVIP. We don't have any details about this killer. In the city of Mumbai, there are number of VVIP, list of which includes top business persons, politicians and Bollywood superstars. We have only one confirmed information that a professional killer has been hired. When we say contract killer, it means, he might be a professional sniper, who can hit the target from a distance of 1000 metres plus distance with 100% accuracy and can conveniently disappear after doing the job. It sounds like the story of 'The Day of the Jackal'. But here we are dealing with the real life killer and not with an imaginary figure."

Abhijeet, who has been listening attentively to Rana says, "Sir, one thing is sure that the killer must be having a proven record as a professional killers, otherwise he would not have been hired by the terrorist group or somebody else. He must be having some contacts in Mumbai to provide him with logistic support. Such professional killers usually don't go on for random killing of people. They always act according to an assigned task and charge exorbitant price for that. Most of the time, it is a difficult task, which warrants proper planning and professional skills. The killer ought to be either an Indian or a Pakistani origin, otherwise it will make him conspicuous and he will get spotted by our law enforcement agencies. This time the challenge before us is more complex and we are dealing with a professional killer, who might have received commandoes training from any of the elite institutes. There are many such examples of professional commandoes getting themselves transformed into professional killers because a single deal can fetch them more than a million."

It's 10.00 a.m. in the morning and Platform No. 1 of Central Railway Station of Mumbai is ready for the arrival of Rajdhani Express from Delhi via Vadodara. It's a prestigious train. Dozens of coolies are waiting eagerly for the train to arrive. Officials of Maharashtra Cricket Association are present to receive the cricket teams of Gujarat and Delhi coming by Rajdhani Express for playing Ranjeet Trophy Cricket tournament matches with the team of Maharashtra. There are lots of cricket fans also present on the platform, who have come to see their favourite players.

When train arrives, the movements of people on the platform get increased. AC first class coaches are the main targets for coolies because they can expect more labour charges from the passengers getting down from the AC first class coaches. Players of both the teams start getting down from the coaches, carrying their suitcases and their cricket kit bags hanging on their shoulders. There are more than fifty persons from both the teams including players, their managers and coaches and they start moving towards the exit gate. In the centre of these people a young man of 28 years of age, putting on a blue colour P-cap, hanging cricket kit on his shoulders and pulling his suitcase is also moving with them. He was smiling and talking to other players pretending as if he is one of them. At the exit point, he shakes hands with two players, but both the players are leading batsmen from different teams. There is a CCTV camera installed at the exit point, which has direct links to various intelligence agencies' control rooms including ATS and they can watch passengers coming out of the station. Security personnel, who are on keen watch, ignored this man. Outside the station, there are two luxury buses parked to take the players and other team members to their respective hotels. That young man with blue colour P-cap takes a taxi and moves from there. The killer has managed to enter the city.

Abhijeet, sitting in the Control Room watches of Exit point of Central Railway station on one of the monitors. His intuition feels that there is something wrong one player shaking hands with other two players of different teams. It means, he is not part of any of the team, then why is he carrying the cricket player's kit.

Abhijeet meets with both the players in the hotels, where the players have been accommodated. Both of them state that they were under the impression that the man is from opposite team. On the basis of description given by both the players, a sketch of the suspect is prepared and circulated to all the police stations.

On 18th floor of a posh residential complex in Chembur, he places his suitcase and cricket player's kit on the table. He goes into the bathroom and removes his moustache with the razor and the long brown colour hair wig. He removes contact lenses and his eye returns to the original grey colour. Now, he is an entirely different personality. He takes out one bigger size suitcase from the cupboard, placing on the bed he opens it. Then he zip opens the kit and transfer different parts of the snipper's rifle into the suitcase. He covers the dismantled parts of the rifle with some clothes and closes the suitcase.

Dialling a number from his mobile he says, "Hello Yunis, Vikrant this side. I am at Chembur flat. What is the latest?"

Yunis in a worrisome voice says, "Yes Vikrant, there is bad news, Police has got your sketch based on the descriptions given by the cricket players. I am reaching at the BPCL petrol pump in the Chembur within 20 minutes. Wait for me near the petrol pump and avoid being noticed."

Vikrant collects the item from the room which may lead to his identity and put them into one of the suitcases. He takes out his loaded revolver and places in the holster under his shirt. Carry both the suitcases out of the room and takes lift straight to the basement car parking. He put his luggage on the back seats of his car and drive out the residential complex. The moment, he comes out of the residential complex, two vehicles of ATS enter in. They miss him by few minutes.

Vikrant shifting his luggage from his car to Mahindra Scorpio of Yunis says, "OK, where are we going now?"

"We have a safer place in Navi Mumbai"

Abhijeet feels disappointed to find that there is no clues left behind in the flat. They find only one empty kit bag, which has been used by Vikrant for carrying the dismantled parts of sniper rifle. The car, which has been abandoned by Vikrant near the petrol pump in Chembur, has all fake papers and fake registration plate. Abhijeet is still hopeful of some clues or witness from the place, where the car has been found abandoned. He put his whole team to find out if there is any witnesses who might have seen the luggage being transferred from the car to some other vehicle.

Abhijeet finds a Honda City, parked on the left side of the car. He call his team members and says, "Look, the vehicle in which the luggage of the car is transferred, must have been parked here, where the Honda City is parked now. This is an area where getting a parking space is a matter of luck and the moment parking space is made available another vehicle occupy it instantly. It means, Honda City owner must have seen the vehicle and its owner in which the luggage was transferred. Let us wait for the owner of Honda City. He may be in a position give some description of the vehicle."

After half an hour, a middle aged man come to open the door of the Honda City. Abhijeet intercepts him and shows him his identity card and say, "Before you parked your car here, there must have been some vehicle, in which some luggage was being shifted from car parked next to your Honda City. Can you give us some details of vehicle and its occupants?"

That man thinking for a moment says, "Yes Sir, when I was searching for a parking space. I saw a person shifting two suitcases in hurry from this car to one black colour Mahindra Scorpio and I thought the Scorpio might leave and there will be space available for my car to park, that's why I stopped my car here. After shifting luggage from the car, the Scorpio moved and I parked my car here."

Abhijeet says, "Did you hear any dialogue between them?"

That man try to recollect and says, "Yes, the person sitting in the Scorpio behind the wheel told another person "Vikrant hurry up" that's all what I heard."

"Do you remember the registration number of the Scorpio?"

"No Sir, my attention was on mainly on space for car parking."

"Can you give us description of their faces?"

"My attention was focused on the man in Scorpio and I saw his face from one side only."

Abhijeet showing him sketch of Vikrant says, "Does another man look like this?"

"No Sir, as far as I remember, he does not look like this. He has no moustache."

"OK, we will appreciate if you please come with us and give us side view description of the man sitting in Scorpio. You can take your car. One of our personnel will accompany you to our HO. Thank you for your co-operation."

Abhijeet calling Rana over wireless says, "Sir, the name of the killer is Vikrant and it appears he has changed his look by removing his moustache. They have moved in black colour Scorpio. The eye witness who has seen his accomplice from one side is being brought to HO for preparing sketch of the second person."

Rana says, "Great, now we are moving in the right direction. I will send an alert for black colour Scorpio and would search profile of Vikrant on our database."

Next day, Rana addressing officers in the conference room says, "We have been able to find the profile of Vikrant. He is an ex-soldier, a trained snipper in the Army and belongs to a farmer's family of district Panipat in Haryana. He participated in number of operations in Army, but due to injuries inflicted by splinters of a hand grenade in J&K, he was declared Medical Category "B" and removed from field operations. On medical grounds he took retirement from Army. After retirement from Army, he could not get job anywhere and ultimately became a contract killer. Two-three assignments in a year could fetch him enough money to live lavish life. Most probably, he has come to Mumbai on contract killing assignment. He is a free-lance killer and does not belong to any terrorist group. Even though this is a case of Mumbai Police, since it has been referred to ATS we will handle it."

He stop for few moments take water and continue to say, "So far as, his accomplice with black colour Scorpio, his name is Yunis. He is a sort of broker between contract killers and prospective customers and takes his cut on such dealings. A team, under Inspector Kanetkar, has already sent to Navi Mumbai to apprehend him."

Rana contacting Kanetkar over mobile say, "Hellow Kanetkar, what is the development?"

"Sir, the flat is locked. Security Guard has informed that Yunis along with one persons has left the building about two hours back. They were carrying one big bag with them while going to the car parking."

Abhijeet gets up from his chair and says, "Oh my God, they have already proceed to accomplish the assignment. We need to flash details of Black colour Scorpio with its registration number to all police check posts to locate it and reach there before it is too late."

Rana says, "I am going to Control Room to flash details of the vehicle. Abhijeet you along with your team go to your vehicles and wait for my message."

Within five minutes, Rana comes on wireless and says, "The Scorpio has been located in Banddra Kurla Complex near a building under construction."

Two ATS vehicles move on for Bandra Kurla Complex.

Vikrant start to takes his position on the 8th floor of the building, which is under constructions, to shoot his target at the exit door of the building which has head office of an International Bank. A business tycoon, who is wearing white suit and expected to come out of the building along with his security guard after his meeting with the Managing Director of the Bank. Vikrant has been contracted for killing of this billionaire businessman, who is running export business of diamonds from Surat in Gujarat. After assembling his rifle and placing it in position, Vikrant assess the distance from window to the exit door of the building from where his target will come out. He make some calculations after taking into account the wind direction and its speed and accordingly adjust telescopic sight of his rifle.

Vikrant keeps on waiting to hear last moment instructions on his mobile about the confirmation when his target appears. After waiting of more than an hour, he sees four persons coming out of the building one out of them is wearing white colour suit. At the same time, he get confirmation over his mobile about the target in white dress. After coming out of the building, they are waiting for their car to come. For Vikrant, who is qualified snipper, a stationery target in the day light is a sitting duck. He fires two consecutive shots, one aiming at the head and second on the chest of the target. He immediately dismantles his rifle, put it in the bag and start to get down through the stairs which have no railings since the building is still under construction. He has hardly got down to the fourth floor, suddenly confront himself with Abhijeet holding gun in his hand. Vikrant drops the bag and try to pull his revolver from the holster, but he is no match to Abhijeet and four bullets from the hand gun penetrate his chest. Vikrant falls from the fourth floor on the ground floor where scrap steel rods also pierce through his body.

On the basis of statement of Yunis, a rival diamond businessman from Surat is arrested by Police. Abhijeet feels regret for his failure to prevent the killing.

CHAPTER - IX

Rana calls Abhijeet to his chamber and says, "Mumbai Police has referred a case of serial extortions of money by a gang operating within the city. They are usually targeting big builders and demand Rs.10 crores onwards. Here is the file forwarded by Mumbai Police. Chief has directed that the case to be handed by our team."

Abhijeet opening the file says, "You must have gone through the file. What is their modus operandi?"

Rana, giving slight turn to his chair rightward so as to face Abhijeet, says, "Unlike other extortionists, these people first give threat over phone and demand money and in case their target does not fulfil the demand they kidnap any of the family members to exert pressure. In two cases, where the police was involved, they have executed the captives. That's it."

Abhijeet in a thoughtful mood says, "Any pending case at the movement?"

"No case at the moment. Hardly, 20 – 30% of such cases are reported to Police for help. Rest of the cases goes unnoticed and the extortion money or ransom is paid by the victims. There is a pattern in their functioning, in most of the cases builders have been targeted."

Abhijeet, reacted as if he gets some clue, says, "It means the culprit is insider of the business of builders. He must be running some leading real estate business, who knows builders' capacity to pay ransom, about their family. Can we have list of such leading real estate agents who have access to leading builders?"

Rana almost jumping from his chair says, "Great Abhijeet, you are genius." He calls head of Data Process wing over intercom and says, "Hello Maniratnam, can you hop in my chamber. There is an urgent piece of work for your boys."

Next moment a South Indian with grey hairs and wearing thick lenses specs enters his chamber and takes seat beside Abhijeet and says, "Yes Sir, hope you have some exciting piece of work for us this time."

Rana with smile explains the whole case to him and say, "We have to shortlist leading Real Estate Agents and Property Dealers of the city, who are friendly with the builders and regularly participating in their social events like marriages, get-togethers and cocktail parties. Our field teams will help you to compile the list and we need it done fast."

Maniratnam, appears confident about the job, says, "It will done Sir. You know Sir, I have always given results to your satisfaction, but being in the supporting service, I have not got any promotion for the last six years whereas my friends working in the field have been promoted twice."

Rana, assuring him, says, "Don't worry, I will speak to the Chief about you, just give me some time."

"Thanks Sir." And he leaves the chamber.

Abhijeet, smiling while going through the file, says, "These supporting services' people are always and everywhere least privileged." He takes the file with him and leave.

After two days, Abhijeet and Rana having gone through many times the comprehensive list of 36 Real Estate Agents and Property Dealers are not able to make out anything from the list.

Abhijeet in his repeated attempts finds some abnormality in case of one real estate agent says, "Sir, look at serial No. 17, Rahul Merchant of Dynamic Real Estate. This guy has started business only four years back and has minted money out of proportion, with his office at Bandara and a four room flat in Lower Parel and also owns a villa in Lonavala. It is most unlikely to make so much money from the number of transactions finalized by him."

Rana's eyes also get widen and says, "Abhijeet, you have again hit the jackpot! You are either too lucky or too genius. Your observation capability is unique!"

"I am simply a professional cop Sir, and trying to learn from you." Abhijeet get blushed with the comments of Rana.

Rana with excitement says, "Great, let us zero in on Rahul Merchant. Put your boys to keep surveillance on his activities. We have to catch him red handed with substantial proof, otherwise he will go scot-free."

Abhijeet looking in the eyes of Rana says in affirmative tone, "Sir, we will demolish his whole network. They are going to spend rest of their life behind the bars."

A group of four Sub-Inspector level officers is called in the conference room. Rana after briefing them about the case say, "You have to keep watch on this man and his accomplices round the clock. Involve as many boys you require but no laps. Now you can proceed." All the four officers salute Rana and move out of the Conference Room.

From next day onwards, Rana and Abhijeet start sitting in the Control Room by rotation so as to monitor the surveillance by their teams on the Rahul Merchant and members of his network, who are running this extortion racket. Identity of all the members has already been established, most of them have criminal records.

On fourth day of their surveillance, Abhijeet get message in Control Room that the gang has kidnapped daughter of Chairman, Ahuja Construction Company Limited, a two thousand crore Rupees organization. Her name is Anjali. While ATS team was trailing a black colour Scorpio SUV, they saw four culprits forcefully pulled the girl from her Mercedes saloon and took her away from the scene.

The Sub-Inspector who is chasing Scorpio comes on the line and says, "Abhijeet Sir, now they are on Mumbai – Pune Expressway and going towards Lonavala. Should we intercept them?"

Abhijeet says, "Don't take any action. Just keep following them at a distance and not to lose trail of them. I am on my way. Most probably they will take her to their villa at Lonavala."

"OK Sir."

Control Room was continuing monitoring the movement of ATS vehicle through GPS. Rana comes to Control Room and say, "Abhijeet you move fast. I will take care of Control Room. All the best Abhijeet. Go ahead!"

Rana addressing to the In-charge of Control Room says, "Use dedicated satellite channel to spot movement of Scorpio and ATS vehicle."

The moment both the vehicles appear on a large size monitor Rana says, "Keep track of both the vehicles."

Rana addressing to the Sub-Inspector Shinde who is chasing Scorpio says, "Hello Shinde, Rana this side. I can watch you through satellite. You are nearing Lonavala. They will take right turn under the highway flyover to reach Villa. Abhijeet has already left and he will be there in next 2-3 hours. Keep strict watch without exposing yourself."

After fifteen minutes Shinde comes on line and say, "Sir, the Scorpio has entered inside the premises of the villa and main gate is closed behind. I am not able to see there moments, however, I am trying to see if there is any activity on the first floor. Wait, wait Sir, I can see through the glass panel of the first floor that the girl, who is blind folded is taken into a room on the first floor."

"Good, keep on watching and keep me informed about their activities. I am approaching Lonavala Police Station to cordon off the area so that nobody can escape from the villa."

Within ten minutes Police In-charge of Lonavala, in civil dress approaches Shinde. All Police force is being deployed in civil dress in the area so as not to create any alarm till Abhijeet arrives.

On reaching at the location, Abhijeet directs three of his commandoes to approach villa from different direction and he himself, holding a bag in one hand, walks up to the main gate and press the call bell. One person comes to the gate and say, "Yes, whom do you want?"

Abhijeet in a very soft gentle way says, "Mr. Rahul has told me to deliver this bag at the villa and take consignment."

The persons inside the villa assumes that he has brought ransom money and open the gate and says, "Get in quickly."

Abhijeet hit the person on the back of his neck and makes him collapse without making any sound. He opens his hand bag, takes out an automatic hand gun and two extra magazines. He moves towards the main door, holding gun, opens the door with a master key and gets inside the house. There is one person sitting on the sofa reading newspaper. Abhijeet gets behind him and in single move breaks his neck. Hiding himself behind the sofa, he tries to assess the situation. There are two persons in the adjoining room sitting at the dining table, taking drinks, eating and laughing. He slowly moves towards the staircase, managing to escape their attention. On approaching first floor, he finds one person sitting on a chair in front of the door, he is carrying revolver in his side holster. From the staircase up to that man there is a distance of about 15 metres. It is not possible to reach him unnoticed and the man can very well create alarm. Abhijeet attaches silencer to his hand gun and fires one shot aiming head of the man, who crumbles down without making any sound.

Abhijeet on opening the doors of the room finds a beautiful girl, with tape affixed on her mouth, sitting on chair. She gets scared to see gun in his hand. Abhijeet lowering his gun gets closer to her saying, "Listen Anjali. Don't get scared. I am DSP Abhijeet from ATS. I have come to rescue you. Don't make any noise, we are not yet out of danger. OK."

He removes tape from her mouth. Before taking her out, he makes sure that it's clear outside. Both comes down the stairs. When they were moving towards the doors to come out of the house. Two persons from the adjoining room comes out with guns in their hands. Abhijeet pushes Anjali on the ground and fires quickly, hitting on their foreheads. Anjali gets so scared to see the shoot out that she embraces Abhijeet tightly and starts sobbing. Abhijeet comforting her says, "Relax Anjali, now you are safe. Soon you will be with your family."

Abhijeet sends message for his team to get in and also informs Rana at Control Room saying, "Sir, she is OK, you may please inform her family."

While local police enters villa, Abhijeet, Anjali and other ATS team members move out of Lonavala, heading for Mumbai. On their way back, she is still holding arm of Abhijeet. First time, he is having different feelings for a lady. He likes it.

When Abhijeet along with Anjali reaches her residence, all family members were already there at the gate. Her father Prem Ahuja receives them. Abhijeet also goes with them inside the villa, which is spread over 2000 sq. metres in a posh area of Mumbai. Mr. Ahuja being a builders has put in all his resources in the construction of his residence. Her two brothers, Mohit and Rohan are also present, beside her uncle and aunty. Mr. Prem Ahuja expressing his gratitude to Abhijeet says, "DSP Abhijeet, you are a brave man. My family will always be indebted to you for saving life of my daughter. I would appreciate if you kindly give me your mobile number."

Abhijeet with all humility says, "It's part of my duty. I can appreciate your feelings, anyhow, you can note down my contact number, but I would request you, no formality please. I will feel embarrassed."

Prem Ahuja jotted down his mobile number on a paper. Anjali along with her father and brothers comes out to see off Abhijeet. Anjali once again holding fast his arm says, "Thanks Abhijeet".

Abhijeet feeling sensation through his body says, "No mention Anjali. You are a very pretty girl." Both the ATS vehicles move for Head Office.

Another team of ATS in a separate raid on the office of Rahul Merchant and took him along with his other accomplice into custody.

Abhijeet sitting in his chamber realizes that he is not able to concentrate on his work and not able to prepare report on the rescue operation of Anjali. He is feeling some sort of restlessness. The whole day he does not talk to anyone and leave office early in the evening. Next day, Rana calls him in his chamber and says, "Abhijeet have you prepared report, the same is required to be forwarded to the Chief?"

Abhijeet with some dullness in his voice says, "It is under preparation, by evening I will submit the same."

Rana, who knows Abhijeet more than anyone else, says, "Are you OK? Tell me, what is the problem?"

"Nothing as such. Since her rescue operation, I am having strange feelings. Don't know, what is this?"

Rana with smile on face says, "I know what it is. You are falling in love with her my dear. Tough commando trainings have supress your delicate feelings. Let these feelings flourish within you. Besides a hard-core commando from MARCOS you are a human also. I wish you success in your love also."

Abhijeet with blush on his face goes back to his chamber to prepare report. Before lunch, he prepares the report and submit the same to Rana. He feels shy going before Rana.

In the evening he receives call on his mobile, he says, "Hello, who is on the line?"

After few seconds caller says, "Hi Abhijeet, Anjali this side. How are you?"

His heart starts throbbing and he says, "I am fine. Hope, you are out of shock now. Nice to hear you."

"Were you expecting call from me?"

Abhijeet manages himself and says, "To be honest I was waiting for your call."

"Abhijeet, can we meet today for dinner at Oberoi Sheraton. I want to give you treat and would also like to discuss on some delicate issue."

"Anjali, what type of issue you want to discuss with me?"

"Abhijeet, let me come straight to the point." There is pause and she continues, "I am in love with you and want to marry you."

"Anjali we will discuss this matter in the evening, we are meeting. I will be there by 8.00 p.m."

"OK, bye Abhijeet, my love."

"Bye Anjali, I love you too." And line gets disconnected.

Abhijeet fails to understand how fast all these development have taken place. He feels quite relieved now. He straightway walks in the chamber of Rana who was taking meeting with other officers. Rana tells them to leave. Looking into the eyes of Abhijeet says, "What happen?"

Abhijeet says, "Sir, Anjali called me and have invited me for dinner tonight."

"Abhijeet, you are telling me half the story. What else did she tell you?

"Sir, she says," hesitatingly he continues, "She says, she loves me and want to marry."

"And you said, you love her too."

"Yes Sir, how do you know?"

Rana laughs and says, "I have passed through this stage long back. Go there well dressed and take a good bunch of flowers for her."

Abhijeet with smile on his face leaves for home to get ready for dinner. He is too excited to meet her.

When he enters lobby of Oberoi Sheraton, Anjali in her maroon costumes, holding same colour purse in one hand was sitting on a far end sofa. She was looking gorgeous with her slim body with curves, oval shape face, wide sexy lips and with dimples on her both cheeks when she smiles. Both walks towards each other in the lobby. For the last few steps, she moves fast and hug him, closing her eyes says, "I love you Abhi".

Abhijeet also whispers, "I love you too, Anju". Oblivious of the people sitting in the lobby, they keep on hugging each other for few moment.

Separating from each other, but holding hands firmly, she leads him and say, "Let us go to Fenix restaurant."

While sitting at the table reserved for them, he places the bunch of flowers on the table and says, "This for my love."

Anjali admiring the bunch of flowers says, "Thanks Abhi." She unexpectedly kisses him. He could feel the soft and warm touch of her lips on his lips and gave her long kiss. They settle down on the sofa sitting closely with each other. Both were looking in each other's eyes, unaware of a waiter, who is awaiting to take order from them until the waiter says, "Yes Sir".

Anjali places order and says, "One Krug Brut Vintage Champagne and assorted chicken as starter."

Waiter bring a bottle of Krug Brut Vintage holding in a wine cooler, places two wine glasses on the table, opens the bottle with corkscrew, pours champagne in each glass, put the bottle back in the wine cooler which is filled with ice cubes.

Anjali handing over one glass to Abhijeet and taking one for herself says, "Let us today, celebrate beginning of our love life with my favourite drink. Cheers Abhi, long live our love life."

Abhijeet, lifting the glass says, "Cheers for our love Anju."

They toast their drinks, clinking glasses of each other's. Anjali presses his hand and says, "I love you so much. Can't sleep for the last two days. Whole night, I keep on dreaming about you. When are you going to marry me?"

Abhijeet caressing her hand says, "What about your family? Are they ready?"

Anjali says, "Yes, I have talked to my Papa. He is very happy to know. He wants to talk with you. Can you make it for tomorrow? I really can't wait any more. I have already accepted you as my husband in my mind and heart."

"Relax, fix up time with your Papa for tomorrow. I too can't live without you."

Waiter again comes to fill their glasses with drink and says, "Would you like to order for main course now, please."

Anjali says, "Sure, bring chicken biryani with less spices, mixed veg raita, salad followed by butter scotch ice cream. That's all."

Abhijeet who is watching the way she is placing order, says, "You seem to be fond of typical Indian dishes."

When waiter brings bills, Abhijeet tries to make the payment, but she interrupts and says, "The first treat from my side." She laugh and says, "Rest of the life you are going to bear me, but don't worry. Now you are part of the Ahuja family, of course you will have full dignity of yours."

Abhijeet is impressed by the way she conducts interaction with him and says, "Anju, your maturity level is so high. I can appreciate it. Let us move. I will drop you at your residence."

She holds his muscular arm firmly and walk out of the hotel. Abhijeet sits in Mercedes saloon with Anjali and tells his driver to follow the car. All the ways, she keeps on holding his arm. On arriving at her residence, Abhijeet ask driver to stop car outside, gets down, she also comes out saying, "Abhi, with you I feel myself safe and protected."

Abhijeet, holding her hand says, "Just wait for some more time. I am always there with you. OK, I will come tomorrow. Good night Anju."

Anjali helplessly says, "Abhi, I can't kiss you on this moving road and that too in front of my house. Don't go please. Want to spend some more time with you!"

"Have patience, Good Night Anju. Bye!" Releasing her hand he moves to his vehicle. Though, he is willing too to spend some more time with her, but with reluctance moves from there. When he turns to look back, she is still standing there. Both wave their hands to convey good bye. Sitting in the vehicle, he thinks *She has gone mad for him, but same is true with him.* A broad smile comes to his face.

It is a spacious drawing room with luxurious sofas lying there with enough capacity for 30 persons to sit at a time. There are four designed centre tables placed for serving to the guests. It is almost a big hall, a cream colour sliding curtain is there to bifurcate the hall. One side is being used as drawing room and another side accommodates a long dining table. The curtain slides through a remote controlled electronic device when the guests, sitting in the drawing room, have to take lunch or dinner.

On two rows of drawing room all family members of Anjali including her parents, brothers, uncle and aunty are sitting and talking to Abhijeet, who is sitting in front of them all alone. When Anjali comes, she goes straight to Abhijeet and sits beside him saying, "Hello Abhi."

All family members with smile on their faces watch her. Her younger brother Mohit in a teasing way says, "Anjali, you have changed the side so fast." All family members are amused with this and laugh. But she is unmoved, rather holds arm of Abhijeet, who feels embarrassed.

Mr. Prem Ahuja, who is a seasoned businessman gets sense of Abhijeet being uncomfortable with the action of Anjali says, "Relax my son. You are now our family member." With a gap of few moments he continues to say, "See, I will be very happy, if you both tie the knot. Anjali is only daughter in Ahuja family. We will appreciate if you also join family business in the capacity of a Director. We know your capability, we are confident our construction business will get multiplied. Sky is the limit."

There is silence in the drawing room, perhaps they are waiting for his reaction to the proposal. Prem Ahuja continue to say, "It is not our condition. We wish to induct you in the family business, which has tremendous scope for expansion."

Abhijeet, who has been listening to Prem Ahuja, with all humbleness says, "It is so kind of you that you have found me worthy of such a big responsibility. I have served force in the capacity of commando for more than four years, which is considered a life span for a professional commando to work in the field. I was already thinking for a suitable profession where I can apply my full potential. I don't think there can be a better opportunity than your proposal." He pauses for a moment and then with the gesture of his hands says "That's all, I have to say."

Prem Ahuja get up and embraces Abhijeet. All other family members also get cheered up. Anjali's elder brother Rohan's wife, Manju brings two red colour jewellery boxes, containing two gold chains. She gives one lady's chain with diamond pendulum to Abhijeet and one thick heavy gent's gold chain to Anjali and says, "OK, what are you waiting for you love birds, go ahead."

Abhijeet and Anjali both put chains to each other's neck. All family members start clapping and chanting, "Congratulations to Abhijeet and Anjali". All family members, turn by turn, offers sweet to both of them.

Prem Ahuja says, "I will talk to Panditji for a suitable dates for formal engagement ceremony and marriage.

Abhijeet, you can inform your family. All the arrangements for their stay and function will be done."

Abhijeet looking to Anjali says, "Happy?"

She smiles and holding his arm fast says, "Yes, today, I am on top of the world and the happiest person on the earth." She continue to hold his arm. Abhijeet likes it.

All family members are overjoyed since they have not only found a perfect match for Anjali, who has saved her life, but also an invaluable asset for their business empire, who will take it to new heights.

Abhijeet and Anjali meet everyday evening on week days either in a five star hotel for dinner or he comes to her residence "Ahuja Sadan".

"Ahuja Sadan" is a six storeys building with two basement. Upper basement being car parking and lower basement used as stores. First floor is for Mr. and Mrs. Prem Ahuja and shared by Anjali. Second Floor for Rohan and his wife, which is also shared by Mohit, who is still unmarried. Third and fourth floors is reserved for Mohit and Anjali respectively when they get married. Fifth floor is meant for guests. The sixth floor is used as Office and other business purposes. On top of the building, there are few rooms for servants and guards. And it also accommodate one heavy duty electricity generator and AC cooling plant since the building is centrally air conditioned. There are three lifts, two for family members and the third is used by servants and guards. Main kitchen is on Ground Floor, though all floors have provision of kitchen. There are many CCTV cameras installed for security purposes. State of art communication system has been installed for each room of the building. Fourth floor is being refurbished on priority since Anjali is getting married and after marriage they will occupy this floor.

In a grand function at Oberoi Sheraton, where more than 1000 dignitaries from business community, ATS and other sections of the society were invited, takes place for the marriage of Abhijeet and Anjali. Chief Minister of the State is also present to bless the newlywed couple.

After function, Abhijeet and Anjali take Swiss Air's flight to Switzerland for couple of weeks to enjoy the best moments of their honeymoon.

CHAPTER - X

Corporate Office of Ahuja Construction Co. Ltd. is located in "Ahuja Tower", a fifteen storeys at Mindspace complex, Malad. It consist of HR, Finance, Architectural, Project Planning and other administrative wings of the Ahuja Group. Group, being in the construction business of residential and commercial complexes, have tried to showcase their professional abilities of architecture, design and construction in the building "Ahuja Tower".

Abhijeet, after getting relieved from the Police Services of Maharashtra, joins Ahuja Group. Mr. Prem Ahuja, Chairman addressing all Directors and Head of Different Departments in the Board Room on 9th Floor, says, "I am glad to introduce my son-in-law, Mr. Abhijeet Kamat as Director (Projects). He comes from a senior position from ATS with meritorious records, which is known to all of you. With his proven ability to perform and to deliver results, I am confident he will take Ahuja Group to new heights and will enhance Group's business by many folds." Addressing to Abhijeet he says, "Abhijeet please,"

Abhijeet stands up and all greet him with applauds. He says, "Thank you very much for entrusting with this responsibility."

All Directors of the Company and HOD shaking hands with Abhijeet congratulate him on his induction as Director (Projects).

In the Chairman's Office, Rohan, Mohit and Abhijeet are sitting in front of a grey colour table. Prem Ahuja, sitting on the other side, resting on the back of his chair addresses them and says, "Abhijeet, for the initial six months, you will be attached to me and participate in our all business meeting so that you will have first-hand idea of our corporate working. Mohit will take you round the office to introduce with other senior officers of the Group at HO. He will also explain you about functioning of different sections. Rohan will take you to our different projects sites and you will be spending ten days at each site so that you will be able to understand the functioning of our construction business."

Prem Ahuja along with Rohan and Mohit leads Abhijeet to his new office, which has his name plate affixed at the entrance. Prem Ahuja ushering in Abhijeet says, "I wish you all the best for beginning of your new career. I am sure, you will prove worthy of this business, which is full of challenges. Abhijeet, you may go ahead with your work now. Rohan and I have to rush for a meeting with Banker. Mohit will remain with you to introduce you with your staff and others."

Abhijeet, while going through the brochures of the Group is surprised to see Anjali entering his chamber holding a bouquet of flowers. Giving him a hug, she says, "Congratulations Abhi for beginning of your new assignment."

"Thanks Anju. I was missing you a lot. Your presence will give me lot of strength."

"I am always with you, Abhi. Hope, you like this place. Soon you will get used to new environment, which is different from ATS, but it carries more and bigger challenges at every steps. Soon, you will get to know. We all are there to assist you in your new venture."

"Anju, so long you are with me, I can face any challenges on the earth."

Anjali with smile on her face says, "Oh, is it so?"

Mohit, so has been watching them, says, "Anjali, now let us do some business. If it is over, please."

Anjali with disappointment says, "Mohit, you are so damn boring. OK Abhi see you in the evening. Try to come early."

Mohit interrupting her says, "Hey Madam, now he is Director (Projects). Forget, he is not coming home before 9.00 p.m."

Anjali defying Mohit says, "Mohit, once you get married, I will take full avenge. I will not even let you talk to your sweetheart. Do you get me?"

Abhijeet feels amused with the skirmishes of brother and sister and says, "OK, Anju relax now. I will try to come early. Happy?"

With the every passing day, Abhijeet's involvement in the business activities increases and he devotes more than 15 hours a day either in the office or at the project sites. His positive and firm attitude and the way he conduct himself have earned him appreciation from all. Whenever he speaks it carries depth and people respect him.

Prem Ahuja addressing Board of Directors in a special convene Board Meeting says, "I am glad to inform the Board of Directors that your Group has been awarded construction work of Residential, Commercial and Office complexes with total contract value exceeding Rs.30,000 crores for the proposed Smart City, which is coming up along the Mumbai – Pune Expressway. This Smart City is going to be the first greenfield smart city project in the country. Despite a tuff competition from international companies, your Group, in joint venture with a leading Korean Company, has been able to bag this prestigious project, which has placed your group amongst the top 100 construction companies of the world. I congratulate all Directors, Officers, Staff and Workers of Ahuja Group."

Everybody stand up and give long applaud almost for one minute. Prem Ahuja continuing his address says, "It is most challenging project, which needs all out efforts using our all resources. I am further pleased to inform Board of Directors that Mr. Abvhijeet Kamat will be responsible for overall project co-ordination and execution, which is the most challenging aspect of these projects. I am confident that our project team under the leadership of Mr. Abhijeet will be able to complete these projects ahead of scheduled period of five years from the date of commencement of work for which we have six months for mobilization of our resources at the site and the countdown for that has already started. We have to get to work fast. The project work will go on round the clock and seven days a week. I once again congratulate all of you. Thanks."

Once again there is a big applaud by all present in the Board room.

Same evening, at 6.00 p.m., Prem Ahuja taking a meeting of senior Executives of the Group, wherein, besides Abhijeet, Rohan and Mohit representatives of Korean company are also present to decide further course of action. Prem Ahuja addressing the more than twenty persons says, "Although, the Maharashtra State Road Development Corporation (MSRDC) has already acquired more than 1500 hectares of land, but local leaders are creating hurdles. As per the Feasibility Report prepared by the Consultants, layouts of the infrastructures, residential and commercial complexes to be created in the Smart City are already decided. Laying of sewer & water pipe lines is being done by separate agencies. Construction of road networks is also progressing."

He continue to say, "Details of manpower, machines & equipment required for each site of the project are already available with us. Some specialized construction equipment, electronic appliances to be installed will be arranged by our Korean Joint Venture Partner and remaining resources need to be arranged by us. Not many construction equipment can be spared from our other project sites. Rohan, you can go ahead with your presentation for procurement of equipment and machines."

Rohan starts presentation through his laptop, which is connected to a large digital screen and says, "Within six months of commencement of construction of high rise commercial and residential towers, we will require fifty tower cranes having large size booms with concrete placement attachments for the first phase and additional fifty tower cranes in next six months. So far, we have received confirmation for the supply of only twenty tower cranes of required specifications. We need to tie up with overseas supplier for the remaining thirty tower cranes for each phase. The quantum of float glasses required for all types of building compledes is more than one million square metres, which makes it another critical item, which needs to explore sources of supply while maintaining the cost factor within the limits. We have already floated global query for the supply of float glasses. For other construction machinery and equipment representatives of Indian and overseas suppliers will start coming from tomorrow for negotiations and finalization of the orders. Approval of Hon'ble Chairman will be taken for all major orders."

Prem Ahuja says, "Myself and Abhijeet will go to Europe next week and will meet with Tower Crane manufacturers in Germany and Switzerland."

Prem Ahuja addressing to Abhijeet he continues to says, "Can you get as many officers from ATS, who may be willing to have their career in our organization. They will get good packages and other facilities. We need them for creation of security network for our project sites in Smart City."

Abhijeet says, "Definitely, many close confidants of mine have approached me for suitable opening in our Company. I will call them. One thing more Sir, I have seen tower cranes lying idle with many builders. Those, in good working condition, may be either purchased from them or taken on hire till we receive cranes from the suppliers."

Prem Ahuja appreciating the idea says, "That's a good idea, you can talk to them and get them checked and evaluated through our Mechanical Engineers. Many builders will be willing to dispose of tower cranes lying idle." He continue to says, "Construction camps at the project location must start within a weeks time and accommodation for all categories, dining halls with proper cooking arrangements, site offices, makeshift hospital and guest house must be completed in three months. Before starting these construction these facilities, please show me the drawings. Assign these works to sub-contractors."

Addressing all present in the conference room Prem Ahuja says, "Every Saturday evening a Review Meeting will be taken by Abhijeet and copy of minutes of the meeting be sent to me. The review meeting should cover all aspects including Manpower, order and delivery position for equipment and machines, status of financial tie up, construction power for the site, camp constructions and statutory clearances. The Project site will have helipad for landing of helicopters, which will be used for VIPs and for our own visits to save time."

Addressing Abhijeet he continue to say, "Abhijeet, you can carry on with the meeting. I have to take flight for

Singapore. There is a meeting scheduled for tomorrow with the Managing Director of Barclays Bank."

SP Rahul Rana joins Ahuja Group as President to look after Security, general maintenance, horticulture, general transport vehicles and cars of the group for all project sites. Though, he was senior to Abhijeet in ATS, but in this organization he will be reporting to Abhijeet.

Abhijeet addressing to Rana, says, "See, we have to put barbed fencing around our all construction sites at the project, create check posts at entries and construct observation tower at every 100 – 200 metres along the fencing, suitable lighting to be installed to prevent pilferages."

Rana says, "Fencing work at all the sites of the project have commenced, but we are facing some resistance from the locals. It seems they are being instigated by some local leaders. They want to talk with the Management of the Company only to settle their issues."

"You may call their leaders tomorrow to our Head Office in the evening, Mohit, you and me will talk to them. Arrange company's vehicle to bring them to the office and treat them well. If possible, find out background of each of their leaders. Put some Security Inspectors, who have joined from ATS on this job because they know how to gather information regarding someone."

Three local leaders from different locations adjoining the proposed Smart City come for meeting at the Head Office. Abhijeet addressing them in the conference room says, "My name is Abhijeet Kamat and I am Director In Charge for the Smart City Project, which will create lot of job and business opportunities for the residents of your regions. The state of art facilities with regard to medical and education will come up in your region. I seek your co-operation for execution of the project. You can tell me frankly, what can we do for the welfare of your people?"

One of the leaders says, "Sir, we know you very well and have heard great stories about your bravery. That is why we have come to you with hope."

"Come on, now tell me what are your issues?"

One of the leaders manage to says, "Sir, we are poor tribal and our people will never be able to afford the education and medical facilities of your Smart City. We don't have proper arrangement for drinking water and sanitation. We don't want assurances of jobs for your unemployed young people, we want jobs in the project work."

Abhijeet appreciating their view point says, "Your problems are genuine. Let your all unemployed young boys come to our site office. We will give them job as per their merit and will also give them training. Regarding education and medical facilities, if you can arrange to make land available in your villages, our company will pay cost of the land, construct and run schools and clinics free of cost. We also promise to construct temples in your respective area. We will also create facilities for water and toilets in your areas. Now tell me what else do you want?"

The leaders look at each other, but could not dare to speak. Abhijeet is able to sense their reservations and says, "It is OK, it will be between you and us, you can meet Mr. Rana every month to collect your packets. I hope, now all issues are taken care and with our proposal for jobs, schools, clinics and temples, your people will be happy."

"Thanks Sir." All the three leaders spoke in one voice, get up, and bow before Abhijeet as a token of respect and leave.

"You are so generous, I like it." Mohit says.

Abhijeet says, "We have to avoid confrontations with the local people, because it is a sensitive area. Their problems are genuine. Once their people get employment to earn livelihood and free education & medical facility, they will be loyal to the organization instead of creating any problems. Moreover, I strongly believe, we must pay back to the society."

A Television team has come to interview Abhijeet regarding proposed Smart City. When camera start rolling, the Anchor says, "Mr. Abhijeet, since you are the Director In Charge for the construction of Residential and Commercial Buildings complexes in the Smart City, will you please tell us the name of the city and highlight the features of the proposed city for the benefit of our viewers."

Abhijeet looking at the camera says, "The name of the city is 'Maratha City', which is going to be first greenfield smart city, which means starting from scratch, in the country. It is going to be a commercial and financial hub with global connectivity, which will boost economy of the State and nation as well. High rise buildings are being constructed with a view to create high density of population. Buildings are designed keeping with an objective to improve energy efficiency. Sensors will be embedded in the buildings for safety of the residents. With the use of Information Technology in residential and commercial buildings use of internet and communication will improve. Solid waste will be disposed of through pipes using vacuum system through tubes. There will be parks and green patches along all the roads. A network of monorails has been planned, which is being executed by a separate agency, for mass rapid transportation of people. This will reduce emission of greenhouse gases."

"How are you going to complete this project of this magnitude in a stipulated time of five years?"

"The Korean Company, who are our joint venture partner, are providing us with technical know how to construct buildings in much shorter period and they will supply and install electronic devices, lifts, elevators for all residential and commercial buildings."

"Are you constructing residential complexes for lower segment of the society also?"

"Yes, there will be residential complexes for all category. The concept of the smart city is to provide affordable housing facilities and job opportunities for all that is why high density residential complexes along with financial and commercial complexes have been planned."

"Thank you very much Mr. Abhijeet." With this the interview concludes

It is now more than one year since the project works have commenced at the proposed Smart City. Hundreds of buildings, which are under constructions, have mushroomed all over the region covering 1500 hectares of land. Many buildings have even attained more than ten storeys levels superstructures and they have yet to go another forty storeys. There are thousands of heavy duty construction equipment & machines and more than twenty thousands workers deployed at the project sites. Arranging for boarding & lodging for such huge workforce is itself a major task. Abhijeet is very particular about the welfare of the workers. At the same time, he does not allow any nuisance in the project area. He personally participate in all religious festivals like Holi or Ganpati Puja.

Abhijeet, most of the time, remains at the project site. He is always busy either having meetings or visiting one building to another building which are under constructions. He always attend to his staff, workers or officers, whosoever comes to him for any problems, whether personal or related to works, and he resolves their issues by taking instant decision. Everyone is happy under his leadership. He works nonstop, but never gets tired. Workers and Engineers get handsome incentives for the progress done by them beyond their monthly targets. They are striving to attain maximum progress to earn more incentive.

There are many articles being published in media and TV channels giving lot of coverage about the progress of Smart City. Chief Minister, during his site visit, has admired the progress of the work. Rates of the property in Smart City have shot up in anticipation of an early completion of the project.

Prem Ahuja, addressing the Annual General Meeting of the Shareholders says, "I am pleased to inform you that your company has achieved commendable progress at Smart City project. We are going ahead of the schedule and will establish new benchmarks in the construction history. All this is possible due to the efforts and leadership of Mr. Abhijeet Kamat, who is Director In Charge of the Project. I am further pleased inform you that in recognition of the outstanding performance by Mr. Abhijeet Kamat, the Board of Directors of the Company have decided to promote Mr. Abhijeet Kamat as Managing Director of the Company with immediate effect." All shareholders and Directors applaud for Abhijeet.

With Abhijeet's elevation to the position of Managing Director of the company, his responsibilities have also increased. Now he has to look after all other project sites of the Group in addition to Smart City project and will not be able to devote his full time for this project. He decides to delegate responsibilities to competent young executives and promoting them to the position of President in their respective field of operations. He keeps in touch with them through video conferencing whenever he is away from the site.

Rana sitting in Abhijeet's office says, "Abhijeet, you have transformed yourself from a Super Commando into a business tycoon in a short span of two years. What a transformation!"

Abhijeet's mother-in-law calling from the maternity hospital says, "Hello Abhijeet. Congratulations, you are blessed with a son."

Printed in the United States
By Bookmasters